Thanks

Pablo Katchadjian

THANKS

A Novel

Translated from Spanish by
Priscilla Posada

DALKEY ARCHIVE PRESS

Originally published in Spanish by
Blatt & Ríos (Argentina) as *Gracias* in 2011.

Copyright © by Pablo Katchadjian, 2011.
Translation copyright © by Priscilla Posada, 2019.
First Dalkey Archive edition, 2019.
All rights reserved.

Library of Congress Cataloging-in-Publication Data

Names: Katchadjian, Pablo, author. | Posada, Priscilla, translator.
Title: Thanks / Pablo Katchadjian ; translated from Spanish by
Priscilla Posada.
Other titles: Gracias. English
Description: First Dalkey Archive edition. | McLean, IL :
Dalkey Archive Press, 2019.
Identifiers: LCCN 2018026160 | ISBN 9781628972955
(pbk. : acid-free paper)
Classification: LCC PQ7798.421.A83 G7313 2018 | DDC 863/.7—dc23
LC record available at https://lccn.loc.gov/2018026160

www.dalkeyarchive.com
McLean, IL / Dublin

Printed on permanent/durable acid-free paper.

CHAPTER 1

I HAD BEEN waiting for two hours in the wooden cage along with the other two hundred slaves. The port seemed both unknown and familiar to me; I wanted to ask the man next to me for the island's name, but he appeared to have fainted, and when I turned around I saw that he wasn't the only one to have done so. Suddenly, they opened the cage and those of us who were fine went out to some steps. They took me right away because I was in good health and looked nice, according to my buyer, a fifty-something-year-old man, bald, pleasant, not too tall, and a little fat, named Anibal. We got in his car and he took me to his house, a castle built on a hill. From my room's window, I could see the port as a miniature; that evening I spent hours contemplating and drinking and eating what a very old and stooping servant kept fetching for me every so often. Following Anibal's warning, I went to sleep early: he had told me that a very long workday awaited us.

I woke up with breakfast at my side: tea with toast and cheese. I drank the tea and ate the toast with the cheese; then I looked at the sky through the window and noticed

3

it was almost noon. I was in my underpants, and suddenly a young and very pretty servant entered. When she saw me, she blushed and said, looking at the floor, that the master, Anibal, was waiting for me at the castle entrance with the dogs and the armaments. "Okay," I said, intrigued and also a little embarrassed over my nakedness. "Do you need anything?" she asked. "Yes, some clothing." "Ah, of course, sorry, I forgot," she replied, and handed me a package that she had in her hands, and which I hadn't seen. "And my old clothes?" I asked, just to say something. "Ah, we had to throw them away, they were very dirty and smelled bad." "Of course, I can imagine." "May I go?" she asked, and I told her yes while thinking no, I would have liked for her to stay and for us to spend the day in bed, since, not counting a very savage and unpleasant episode in the slave cage, sex had been absent from my life for a few months now, let alone love and tenderness. And this servant, who told me her name was Ninive before leaving, seemed sweet. While I dressed, I imagined a life with Ninive in a humble but comfortable house at the foot of a mountain; this thought was interrupted by a shout from Anibal from the castle entrance—which, I noticed in that moment, was just below my window—: "Let's go already, the dogs are getting antsy!" I looked out and shouted that I was coming down, and was really surprised by the number of dogs, about fifty of them.

As soon as I went outside, Anibal embraced me and told me that I looked even nicer than the previous day, and to please pick a rifle. He already had his. There were five rifles lying on the ground; I took each one and tried the scope and adjustments; they were all good, but for some reason, I liked the one painted red. "You like that one?" asked Anibal. "Yeah, I think so." "Ah, let's see . . . ," he said and took it away from me. He did what I did with the scope and adjustments; then he hung it over his shoulder, said, "All right then," and gave me his: "You'll be fine with this one, I'll keep the red one." "Sure, no problem." "Of course there's no problem," he replied with a smile. Anibal's rifle was much better than the red one I had picked, but I didn't say anything. "What's the plan?" I asked him. "I don't know, we're going hunting, what do you think?" "Hmm . . ." "What? What's wrong?" "I don't know, I always feel a little bad when I kill animals needlessly." "Yes, it's true . . . but do you have any better ideas?" I thought for a while: "No, the truth is I don't." "Good, so let's go. If we don't kill anything it doesn't matter, it's a sport." "Yes, of course." "In fact," he insisted, "let's not shoot to kill." "Good, that's better." We each mounted a horse and rode off followed by the dogs. I wanted to blow a kiss to Ninive, who was watching me from my bedroom window, but couldn't summon up the energy, and thought that a different man with a different personality would have done it, and that this act could have easily been the beginning of something.

Once in the forest, Anibal stopped his horse and, without getting off, started shooting in every direction, in a ridiculous manner that included closing his eyes a bit. He made me think of a man who . . . I thought that he would stop soon, but he kept on like that for a few minutes, reloading bullets every so often, and only stopped when he was defeated by his own panting. He dismounted his horse, left his rifle on the ground, and for a good while remained bent over, with his hands on his knees. Then he looked around, said,

"Such bad aim," and started laughing like crazy; he took a few steps and grabbed three dead birds; then, still panting, pointed at me and said: "Now you!" "What?" "Now it's your turn!" "Turn for what?" "Shooting, what else?" I stayed quiet. "What's wrong?" he asked, a little annoyed. "No, nothing." "Good, so shoot, that's why we're here." I got nervous and could only say: "We came to hunt?" "Yes, of course, I got three birds, now it's your turn." "But I prefer shooting little by little, carefully." "No! Shoot now!" "But all the animals were scared away . . ." "No, none of that!" "It'll be a waste of ammunition." "I'm the one paying for ammunition! Shoot!" I fired three shots into the air and looked at him. "That's nothing! Shoot for real! Forty shots in a row!" "No, let's walk a little and shoot as we go, aiming at animals." Anibal mounted his horse and pointed at me with his rifle, laughing: "I thought you didn't want to kill animals . . . Shoot!" Then I began shooting timidly, very slowly, but when I saw Anibal's face I realized that it was in my interest to do it right, so I started jumping on the horse firing shots into the air, and soon I noticed that I was doing it enthusiastically, so I kept on like that and reloaded the rifle over and over again, and all of a sudden I had contracted Anibal's laughing fits. I don't know how long this went on, but I could have gone on for much longer if Anibal hadn't stopped me. "What? What?" I asked him, agitated. "Nothing, we're done, relax. Look, you did well." From atop the horse I looked around; there were monkeys, birds, some larger fowl, and even an animal with horns. All dead. "What happened?" I asked. "Nothing, everything went well. Let's collect this mess." "No, no . . ." "Get down and help me." So, I got down; I thought that upon gathering the animals I would feel disgust and guilt, but that wasn't the case: we did the work laughing and chatting. Anibal told me that he was a widower and that he had a son and a daughter. The daughter, who was very beautiful, had married and gone far away, to another island, apparently to get away from him, who was overprotective of her; the son lived in a castle about thirty miles away, and visited now and then. I told him a little about myself. When we finished, we looked at the pile of animals. There were, in addition to the monkeys and the giant fowl, a number of very small felines, and some kind of little horse with three horns. "Good, huh! And the one with the little horns!" he said, and congratulated me with a pat on the back. Two servants, one young and one old, came with a wheelbarrow, and Anibal gave them instructions I couldn't hear, about what to do with the dead animals. The two of us returned to the castle and we said goodbye until dinnertime.

I looked out my room's window and saw the sunset. Activity on the port was winding down. A man washed an almost-empty cage of slaves with a hose. At first I thought it was the same cage that had brought me over, but later I noticed that it wasn't. I thought about those few slaves that remained. If nobody had bought them yet, they surely wouldn't sell. I thought about those slaves rejected by all the buyers and thought about the possible reasons. Farther away, at the border between sky and sea, the Navy trained its sailors to fire cannons.

I was very tired, and so I threw myself on the bed to take a nap, and as I was falling asleep, someone knocked on the door. "Yes?" I said. "It's me." It was a woman's voice. "Who?" "Ninive, who else?" Surprised, I sat down on the bed, grabbed a book that was on the nightstand, and told her to come in. "Hi." "Hi." There was a silence, and then she spoke first: "What are you reading?" "Oh nothing, just a book." "Yes, of course, I see that, but what's it about?" I looked quickly at the cover and blushed. Then she ran over to the bed, snatched the book away from me, and read aloud, with a smile: "*Special Sexual Positions to Practice between Men.*" "I found it here," I said, embarrassed. "Yeah, sure." "Seriously." "Yeah?" "Yeah." "And you like men?" "No, no." "And what about women?" "Yeah, I like women." "Ah." Neither of us said anything; then she asked, "And you like me?" and she ran away before I could respond with anything, laughing manly, little laughs.

I threw myself on the bed again and managed to fall asleep; when I woke up, it had already gotten dark out. The window was open. It seemed to be midnight, and so I assumed I had missed dinner. On the nightstand, where the book on sex between men was still lying, there was a metal dome; the dome had a note stuck on: "Sir Anibal waited for you and you didn't come down!!!!!!" I lifted the dome thinking about the feminine handwriting on the note: there was a steak with mashed potatoes, still warm. I looked at the note again. The letters were very big and happy, clearly female, a little clumsy, and also, it seemed to me just then, childish. I had no doubts that it was Ninive's handwriting. I ate the steak, which was good, and some of the mashed potatoes. Afterward I became thirsty, and since I had no water I went out to look for some in the hallway bathroom. I took advantage of this to pee, and then, seeing there were towels, I got the urge to take a shower. When I was done, I dried myself and, since it wasn't cold at all, I tied the towel around my waist, grabbed my bundle of clothes, and went back to my room. I was about to go in when I heard a woman scream. At first, I decided to ignore it. I went in, got dressed, and sat looking at the book nonchalantly. But the screaming continued, and so I left to find out where it was coming from. I walked down a hallway that appeared to the left. The hallway was curved, and as I moved forward I noticed that the shouts were becoming fainter. So I retraced my steps and turned down a hallway that opened off the middle of the curved hallway. The screaming was more distinct there. It was a woman and a man; the man was Anibal, that was evident; the woman could have been Ninive or not. As I kept walking I was able to hear them more clearly: Anibal was apparently hitting the woman and the woman was crying and begging him to stop, but Anibal laughed and kept at it. After a few more steps, I heard him accusing the woman over a missing chest of gold, and the woman swearing that it hadn't been her and that she knew nothing about the existence of the chest. Suddenly, I heard a door open and Anibal's laughter; I ran back to the curved hallway, took a turn, and made it back to my room. I lay down in bed feeling very disturbed, and since I couldn't sleep, I had no other option but to once again grab the book on homosexual positions, which upset me, above all, because of the drawings.

Chapter 2

THE NEXT DAY, I woke up and saw breakfast on the nightstand. I reached for the kettle and noticed it was warm. I got up and opened the window. It was a pleasant day, neither hot nor cold, and the port bustled with activity. Ships arrived with small cages, of twenty or thirty slaves, and almost always the same thing would happen: a port worker would enter the cage, pick out the sick or unconscious, and take them toward someplace I couldn't see from my window; then the sales were quickly made; sometimes, a man would buy an entire cage, and then, after paying the worker, he would let out the five strongest slaves and make them lift the cage onto a wheeled platform; then these five would pull the platform and slowly guide it along a green path that disappeared into the vegetation.

I returned to the nightstand and poured myself a cup of tea. I ate a little bread with cheese and took a sip of tea. I spent my whole breakfast like that, and just as I was chewing the last piece of bread, Anibal shouted my name from below. I looked out the window and waved to him. "Come down right now!" he shouted. I dressed and went downstairs. Anibal told me that he needed help with something. But having said this he fell silent, so I had to ask him what that thing was. "Well, you know, something trivial." "Okay." Then he told me what it was he needed, and I told him it was fine, that there wouldn't be a problem, though in reality the idea of doing what he was asking me was upsetting. So I spent the whole afternoon doing the job, and as soon as I returned to the castle I showered to clean off the grime that I had stuck all over my body; as much as I scrubbed my hands with a sponge, they remained black; on top of that, a disgusting smell, of decaying fish and death, permeated my hair. It was the smell of humiliation and slavery. I looked out the window, but my eyes, tired and irritated from the heat and gas, prevented me from really seeing anything. Next time, I thought to myself, I'd demand gloves, goggles, and even boots from Anibal.

It was already seven, it had been a long job; I decided to take a stroll to clear my mind. I walked along the grass for a few minutes and sat down in a little grove with my back against a tree. Looking at the tree in front of me, I thought of Ninive, and at that moment I heard a woman scream. I got up and started to look around to see where it was coming from. As the forest grew denser the shouts became louder. Suddenly, I saw Anibal and Ninive. I hid behind a tree and observed them: they were running around as if they were playing, but in reality, I noticed immediately, the one playing was Anibal, because Ninive seemed terrified. Anibal's game consisted in running after Ninive with a stick; each time he caught up with her, he would hit her legs, and she would fall to the ground; then Anibal would let her get up, she would run away again, and he would catch her and hit her again. I kept following them, hiding behind trees, until the moment came when Anibal, instead of letting her get up, threw himself on top of her and started tearing her clothes off. When he was done undressing her, he hit her a little with the stick, half-heartedly, and left. Ninive was left alone, crying. I wanted to get closer, but couldn't summon the courage to do so; I stayed there watching her until she stood up, covered herself a little with her torn clothes, and left.

I returned to my room, closed the door, and immediately there was a knock: it was the old servant, who had come to tell me that Anibal wanted to have dinner with me. I went down to the dining room, feeling a little nervous. Anibal was waiting for me at the table, alone. There were a huge chicken and baked potatoes. Anibal was in an excellent mood; he stood up, embraced me, and invited me to sit next to him. "The chicken is for me," he said; "what do you want?" "Well, chicken would be good." "No, the chicken is for me, and there's no more chicken. Do you want pasta?" "Sure." So then Anibal shouted, "Pasta!" and started savagely eating the chicken. He sullied his face, his hands, his arms, and even his head; every so often, he spit out something he didn't like. When he finished, he stood up and left without saying goodbye. I remained alone at the table, waiting for the pasta, which never arrived.

When I went up to my room, starving and thinking about Anibal with hatred, I found a note from Ninive in which she said that she would wait for me that night in her room and gave me instructions on how to get there. At the end of the note it said: "It'll be fun!!!!!" And under that line there was a horrible little smiley face intended to be friendly; it was more or less like those smiley faces one sees when . . . I wanted to go see Ninive, but I was hungry. And then, probably driven by a sense of smell that I wasn't aware of, and that I could not dispose of whenever I wanted, I opened the nightstand's drawer and found a package of crackers, a piece of cheese, and salami. Underneath the package, there was a very lovely knife, quite big and sharp, with a wooden handle and an interesting shape, soft and animal-like. With the knife, I cut a few pieces of cheese to put on the crackers; then I cut some slices of salami and put them over the cheese. I ate everything; meanwhile, I absentmindedly began using the knife to carve my name into the nightstand's wood. I only realized what I was doing when I finished eating. I covered the markings with the book on sexual positions, grabbed Ninive's directions, and left. I made my way, as instructed, straight down a hallway that ran perpendicular to the one my room was on, and which reminded me of something. Then I came to a closed window and saw the marble staircase beside it; I looked behind me and there was the little metal staircase. I went down carefully and reached a dirt landing; I walked around until I left the castle and, sticking close to its exterior wall, arrived at a metal door painted blue. I entered. It was quite dark and the smell was disgusting. I kept walking until I came to the door with the light; I opened it and found myself inside the castle again; I walked straight and arrived at a curved hallway; Ninive's note didn't say anything about the curvature, and that worried me; at the end of the hallway I arrived at a space like the one outside my room, but different, a little more neglected and decadent; I continued along a hallway, then another, and there a hole appeared in the floor. Something was wrong. I turned around, exited the castle again, entered through another door, reached a wall, opened the wrong door and saw the old servant naked; apologized and turned around; exited the castle, entered through another door, went up a staircase, and arrived in a room full of hunting trophies; I left, frightened, and went into the room next door, which was a library; when I went in, a very young servant who was reading gave a start and stood up, relaxing when she saw it was me: "I thought you were Anibal," she said sighing, and explained, without me asking, how to reach Ninive's room; I turned back and in two minutes arrived at Ninive's door. "You took so long!" she told me, as if angry. "Yes, I got lost." "But you had instructions . . ." "I don't know, I got lost anyway." "Now it's late." "Why? Late for what?" "Anibal will be here any second now." "Anibal?" "Yes," she said, breaking into tears, then she embraced me. I hugged her back, shyly at first, then with a little affection, and Ninive calmed down and told me that yes, Anibal visited her every night and did terrible things to her. "Terrible!" she repeated. "Terrible? What kind of things?" "I can't tell you, they're terrible!" Then we heard a noise and she told me, "run along this hallway," and I left, and very soon arrived back at my room.

I sat on my bed, and almost as a reflex looked at the nightstand: there was a note attached. It was from Anibal, who asked me to do a series of things and gave me instructions, which weren't clear; at the end, it said: "When you see it you'll realize what you have to do." Furious, I crumpled the note and threw it at the wall, but it never made it to the wall because it was so light and I hadn't balled it up tightly enough. That made me even more angry. I shouted like an animal, even if it wasn't very loudly. Determined to finish this assignment as quickly as possible, I grabbed the ball of paper, opened it up, smoothed it out, folded it, and put it in my pocket; I left, grabbed the tools from a little room next to the kitchen, and once outside the castle, I walked in the direction that Anibal had indicated to me in the note. Ten minutes later I arrived at a storehouse. I went in and felt the urge to cry upon realizing what was expected of me. I kneeled on the ground, rested my head against the earth and sang, aloud, the only prayer I had learned as a child: "Please, God, help me to overcome incongruities." When I finished praying I felt a little better and started working like a pig in the middle of the putrefaction. I went very slowly at first, disgusted by the smell; two or three times I vomited, and I believe I fainted one or two times. Nevertheless, little by little, I started to forget what I was doing and began to act mechanically.

Five hours later, with the sun barely peeking out, I returned to the castle. The front door was locked. I went to the back door, but it was also closed, and so I dropped down and slept on the ground. Some hours later the old servant opened the door, woke me up, and had me come inside. When I got to my room I was about to throw myself on the bed, dirty and all, but didn't, fearing I wouldn't be able to change the sheets afterward. So I undressed and took a shower, but the grime didn't completely come off.

CHAPTER 3

THE NEXT DAY, when I opened my eyes, the first thing I saw was my dirty clothing packed in a little bundle next to my bed. I'd dreamed of what I'd done, which I need not exaggerate was a nightmare. I got up and opened the window. It was a pleasant day, neither hot nor cold, and the port bustled with activity. I saw Ninive at the forest entrance; she was accompanied by a servant and pointing to a tree. I grabbed my cheese and crackers and ate a bit. I noticed, while eating, that the cheese had a few green spots; the spots, which I wouldn't have minded any other time, now revolted me, and I stopped eating: in my previous night's work I had seen green spots of all kinds. I went back to the window to take in some air. Ninive and the old servant were returning to the castle. At the entrance, underneath my window, they found Anibal and told him that they had to show him something. "What?" asked Anibal, good-humoredly. "A girl, a dirty girl," replied the old woman. "A girl?" "Yes, a monster-girl. An animal-girl," she insisted. Anibal looked at Ninive and asked her what was going on, but Ninive looked down. "Good," said Anibal, and for some reason looked up and saw me. My first impulse was to hide, and I did, but I immediately returned to absentmindedly look out. "I need your help, something's happened," said Anibal. "I just woke up," I replied, assuming that he would take into consideration the work he had ordered me to do the previous night. "It doesn't matter, get down quickly, and come to the forest." Then I thought that I couldn't wear my previous day's clothing and that I didn't have any other, but, somehow, while I had been talking from the window somebody had come into my room, taken the pile of dirty clothes, and brought me back another pile of clean clothes. Upon grabbing the clean clothing I saw, by contrast, the grime that was stuck all over my body; on top of that, I felt the disgusting smell, of decaying fish, which permeated my hair. It was the smell of humiliation and slavery; my eyes, tired and irritated by the toxic gases, made my vision blurry. When Anibal shouted for me to hurry up, I put on the clean clothes and went down.

I ran to the forest and caught up to them: all three were looking at a treetop. "Shh," said Ninive, with a smile. I looked up; at first I didn't see anything, but then, after a while, a movement caught my attention. "It's a monkey," I said and the three of them laughed. "Shh," said Ninive again. It's an animal-girl, a monster," said the old servant. "A what?" I asked. "It's what is often called a 'wild girl,'" replied Anibal. "Really? A wild girl in the sense of . . . ?" I asked. "Yes, yes, I'm very impressed," he replied. Then I looked and saw more clearly: it was a very dirty and frightened girl. "Go on, come down," Anibal told her in an affectionate tone that gave me goose bumps, but the girl didn't listen. "Let's try something," said Ninive, "you all go and leave the two of us alone." Anibal and I walked a few yards off and watched as the old servant pulled up, with a great deal of delicacy and, one would have to say, wisdom, some roots and gave them to Ninive, who raised herself on her toes, leaning on the tree trunk, and held the roots out to the girl. Then the little black hand reached down and grabbed them. They went on like that for a while, but without any success, because the girl, despite Ninive's persistence and smiles, still didn't want to come down. "Intelligent . . . ," I said, and Anibal looked at me, annoyed. "What's the matter?" I asked him. "You're an idiot." "Why?" "It can't be intelligent, it's like an animal." "And?" "Let's see . . . What's intelligence?" I thought for a while: "I don't know." "So then, don't talk," he told me with contempt and went over to the women. I also headed toward them, with short, quick steps. Anibal said he had to go, but that we should stay there and not let her out of our sight, because he was very interested in the wild girl. He said bye to the women and asked how the stuff from last night had gone. "Good," I said. "Perfect. I'm going into town, do you need anything?" "Town? There's a town?" "Yes, there's a town, of course." "The port?" "No, not the port, the town." "The town? Where is it?" "On the other end of the island." "Which end?" "The port is in the south and the town is in the north." "Oh, I didn't know." "So? Do you need anything? The town is big, they've got everything . . ." And I tried thinking of something, but couldn't, and told him no.

I stayed there with Ninive, the old servant, and the girl in the tree. Ninive told me: "I'm afraid: if we don't manage to get her down and take her to the castle, Anibal will be furious with me." "What do you mean?" I asked. "That Anibal will get mad at me." "But what does he do to you?" "What do you mean 'do to me'? He makes me suffer." "How?" "*How* what? How does he make me suffer?" "Yes." "Why do you want to know?" "I don't know, this situation makes me feel bad." "And? It's not like you do anything to fix it." "No, but . . ." "And on top of that you're sick and want details . . ." "No, no. I want to help you." "How?" "I don't know." "Well, think about it and tell me later." And after saying this, Ninive started circling the tree asking the girl to come down: at first in an affectionate, pleading tone; then angrily, even cursing at her. Determined to try and help her with this, I approached the tree and started to think. When, a few minutes later, an idea occurred to me, Ninive was already horribly cursing at the girl: she was telling her that because of her stubbornness she, Ninive (she said: "I, Ninive"), would suffer a lot that night, and that this type of selfishness disgusted her, because for her, the girl, it would be easy enough to just come down right away. And whenever the old servant hugged her to calm her down, Ninive would push her and throw her to the ground.

The girl remained in the tree, even climbing to a higher branch, visibly very afraid and restless; she moved in such a way that she reminded one of a . . . I ran to the castle and came back with a net and a cage with two live chicks. I told the women to move aside and I hung the net from the branch of a tree next to the tree where the girl was. Meanwhile, Ninive insulted me, the girl, and the old woman. I asked her to calm down and placed a hand on her shoulder; Ninive told me I didn't care about her, that if it was up to me she would have to suffer all her life with Anibal, that she couldn't take it anymore. "Ninive, please, I'm trying to help you." "With this? Do you think Anibal will ever stop? As long as he's alive I will suffer as if I deserved it." "What are you trying to say?" "Nothing, that I can't take it anymore." Disturbed, I returned to my plan. I scattered some corn where the net would fall, freed the chicks who went to eat the corn, and moved aside. We backed away some ten yards and waited. I had a rope in my hand that I'd let go when the girl came down to grab one of the chicks. And so it went, and we trapped her, and although seeing her mutely flail around inside the net made me feel awful, I nevertheless took her to the rear of the castle and locked her in a cage that was next to the kitchen door.

Chapter 4

It was already three. It had been a long job since the wild girl had been slow to come down. After eating a quick snack prepared by the old servant, I went walking along the grass for a few minutes and sat down in a little grove with my back against a tree. Like that, and thinking over what Ninive had told me about Anibal, I fell asleep on the ground. When I woke up it was already dark. I had dreamed something interesting, but couldn't remember it very well; all I knew was that it had nothing to do with anything: it was about a man who sang songs in a theater to an enormous audience; the songs were very modern, but the audience was made up of old people.

I went up to my room, closed the door, and immediately there was a knock: it was the old servant, who had come to tell me that Anibal wanted to have dinner with me. I went down to the dining room. Anibal was waiting for me at the table, alone. There were a huge chicken and baked potatoes. Anibal was in an excellent mood; he stood up, embraced me, and invited me to sit next to him. "The chicken is for me," he said; "what do you want?" "Well, chicken would be good." "No, the chicken is for me, and there's no more chicken. Do you want pasta?" "Sure." So then Anibal shouted, "Pasta!" and started savagely eating the chicken. With a full mouth he congratulated me for having trapped the wild girl and told me that he himself would educate her. "Really?" I asked him. "Yes, yes, I've read a lot about the subject." Then he told me that he had a lot of fun in town, that he had seen a lot of people he knew, and that he had bought me something, and he gave me a package. A little excited, I opened it, and when I saw what it was, Anibal started laughing. "It's a joke!" he said. "I don't get it." "Nothing, nothing, don't get offended," he told me, and took the package from me and threw it at the floor as if it was garbage. Then he stood up and left without saying goodbye. I remained alone at the table waiting for the pasta, which never arrived.

When I went up to my room, starving and thinking about Anibal with rage, I found a note from Ninive in which she told me that she would wait for me in her room and gave me directions on how to get there. At the end of the note, it said: "Please, I beg of you: come have fun with me." As much as I tried, I couldn't find the short path; anyway, I arrived much quicker than the last time. I knocked and Ninive opened the door smiling: "You're late again!" "But much less!" "Yes, that's true . . . Oh . . ." "What's wrong?" "Nothing, just that I would like to spend the night with you, but Anibal will arrive at any moment." "Really?" "Yes, of course." "And what goes on?" "Enough of that!" "It's just that . . . " "What?" "Nothing, that I think about you, and about what he does to you, and . . ." "Don't say anything . . ." "It's just that . . ." And then

Ninive interrupted me and said: "Somebody would have to kill him." "What?" "Somebody would have to kill Anibal." "Do you really mean that?" I asked, with a most likely horrified face and a stupid tone. "No, of course not." "Oh." There was a silence and Ninive said: "Yes, I do mean it." "What?" "That I'm saying it in earnest." There was another silence, very ugly this time, and Ninive said: "No, I don't mean it. Don't take me seriously." "But . . ." "Although at the same time I do mean it." "What do you mean?" "What I'm saying is that you're the one who wants to kill him, but you don't dare." "Me? No . . . that's not true . . ." "It is: you want him to die so we can be together, for him not to do what he does to me anymore, to not make you do those jobs, etc. Before you arrived, everything was fine here and I didn't suffer as much with what Anibal does to me. I could even say that I had a good time, because I didn't like it but it was entertaining. Now everything's changed, and that change is a result of your showing up here." "And that's why I'd have to kill him?" "Yes, of course. And now that you're seriously considering the possibility, I look at you and see a man; and if you did it, you would be even more of a man and nobody would be able to defeat you. Anibal is fat, bald, short. He's worthless. But you're great, and what I'm telling you is to help you take the short path, which entails a little cruelty: in this case, a crime, but a just crime that will bring us all, you, me, and those around us, to a fuller level of justice." ". . ." "Now go, because Anibal, that sadist and slave-driving monster, is about to arrive at any moment." She pushed me and I took off running. I arrived at my room and got into bed. I stayed like that for a few minutes, thinking not only about what Ninive had told me but about how she had said it: those words, those phrases . . . Afterward I got up, grabbed the salami, and nibbled at it without removing the skin. And then I saw a note. It was from Anibal. He was assigning me a job "a little harder than the others," and he clarified that there were boots, gloves, and a helmet so that "nothing ugly" would happen to me. I found a club and set off with the idea of going to Ninive's room and beating Anibal to death, but when I opened the door and went out into the hallway I started to shake. I sat down on the floor and stayed there for a long time, with the club in my hand. Then I stood up, went into my room, left the club, grabbed Anibal's note, went to look for the helmet, gloves, and boots, and spent the entire night in a huge storehouse doing work more repulsive and humiliating than what anyone could imagine; something totally indescribable, impossible to understand if one doesn't see it, and impossible to feel if one doesn't live it. As soon as I returned to the castle I showered to clean off the grime that I had stuck all over my body; even though I scrubbed my hands with a sponge, they remained black; on top of that, a disgusting smell, of decaying fish and death, permeated my hair. It was the smell of humiliation and a darkened life. I felt that I must be the slaviest of all slaves in the world. I lay down and dreamed, even before falling asleep, of variations on Anibal's death.

Chapter 5

The next day, I woke up, saw breakfast on the nightstand, and felt the urge to vomit. I reached for the kettle and noticed it was warm. I got up, opened the window, and saw the wild girl: a rope went from her neck to a stake; the rope was a couple of yards long and that allowed her to run a bit; but when she went too far, the rope choked her. I served myself breakfast thinking about what I had done the night before. I ate a little bread with cheese and took a sip of tea. Then I returned to the window. At the border between sky and sea, the Navy trained its sailors to fire cannons.

It was very early. The day was neither hot nor cold, and the port was full of activity. Ships arrived with small cages, of twenty or thirty slaves, and almost always the same thing would happen: a port worker would enter a cage, pick out the sick or unconscious, and take them away; then, the sales were quickly made; sometimes, a man would buy an entire cage, and then, after paying the worker, he would let out the five strongest slaves and make them lift the cage onto a wheeled platform; then, these five would pull the platform and slowly guide it along a green path that disappeared into the vegetation or down another path that probably led into town. I heard a sound under the window. It was Anibal, who was going out in his car, with the top down, in the direction of the port. I saw him get smaller; for a moment he disappeared, and then reappeared, very small, in the port; his green hat and the odd shape of his car allowed one to identify him. Anibal parked, got out, and approached a cage with about ten slaves. He looked a little and then went off to the side where I couldn't see him. Next, six slaves exited the cage and placed it on a platform. Would he buy more slaves? The idea of living with those ten slaves disturbed me; at the same time, I thought that they could help me with my work and that this would be good. But no: the cage left and Anibal reappeared beside another cage, pointing out a slave. The dockworker brought him out and Anibal examined him. Then I lost him until he reappeared on the path, accompanied by the slave. I heard the voices of women: Ninive, the old servant, and the other young servant, whom I had scarcely seen and now noticed was very pretty, approached the door to wait for them.

I went down too, greeted Ninive with a kiss on the cheek, and said hello to the other two servants. Anibal and the new slave still hadn't shown up. I looked at the young servant and said, "I've never seen you before." She, with a very soft and agreeable voice, replied that we had met, but that she was usually in the library, and then the conversation was interrupted because Ninive grabbed me by the arm and told me she was anxious to see the new slave. "Why?" I asked. "I don't know, to see what happens." "With what?" "We're all anxious," the young servant told me. Then we heard the motor and Anibal appeared with the slave. He was a very ugly guy, big and strong. Anibal got out, opened the door for him, and introduced him: Hugo was his name. Hugo said hello with a very grave and nervous voice. We introduced ourselves and then the young servant took Hugo to his room. Anibal asked me what I thought of the new slave. "I don't know, he's kind of ugly." "Ugly?" "Yes, but it doesn't matter," I said. "And what do you think?" Anibal asked Ninive. "I don't find him ugly; on the contrary, he looks very strong and manly," she replied. Anibal left in fits of laughter.

"What's that about?" I asked Ninive. "What?" "All that 'strong and manly' stuff . . ." "Nothing, just an opinion." There was a silence and I said: "I was thinking about what we talked about yesterday." "Yesterday?" "Yes, what you were saying . . ." "Ah," she said, uncomfortable and feigning disinterest. "Yes, I'm going to do it soon." Then Ninive smiled and told me: "All the same, look, if you're not up for it, don't do it." "No, I'm going to do it." "Well, that's good," she said, as if she didn't care, and left.

After that I went to take a stroll; when I returned to my room, I found Hugo sitting on my bed looking at the book on homosexual positions. "Hi," he said while still staring at the book. "What are you doing here? Are you going to sleep in this room?" "No, no. I wanted to speak with you, Anibal told me that you had to tell me what's done here." "Well . . ." "This book seems interesting," he said. "Yeah? It's not mine." "Oh, it's not?" "No, it was here." "It's good all the same. Can I borrow it?" "Yes, take it." "I have another book in my room, I can lend it to you." "What is

it about?" "I don't know, I flipped through it quickly and it
didn't interest me." "Okay, sure, I'll have a look." "Thanks,"
he said. "No, it's fine." There was a silence and Hugo told
me: "The servant's pretty." "Which one?" "I don't know her
name, it's a weird one." "Okay, but which one? The one who
took you to your room?" "Yes, of course, the other one is
ugly." "Which one's ugly? The old one?" He laughed: "Well,
the old one is old. The other one is ugly. The pretty one is
the one who accompanied me. Are you involved with her?"
"No, no." "Ah, perfect, because we were messing around on
my bed, you know . . ." "Really!? Already?" "Yes, you know
. . . I grabbed her, gave her a little push, and she gave in. We
had a good time, shouted a lot." "Ah . . . I didn't hear anything . . ." "No, you're far from my room. And you? Are you
with someone?" "I befriended Ninive, the one you think is
ugly." "Ah, sorry." "No, no worries. I had never seen yours.
Still, I like Ninive more." "Really?" "Yes." "Well, different
tastes." "Yes, of course." "Still, now that you mention it, that
Ninive isn't so ugly." "I think she's pretty." "Yes, perhaps . . .
And you haven't . . ." "No, no, we have something, but she's
a bit hysterical . . ." "Ah, of course. You've got to be firm . . ."
"Perhaps . . . Well, should I explain what we do here?" "Go
ahead, yeah." So then I told him about the work I had had to
do and saw how his good humor started to fade. When I finished, he told me: "I've never done anything like that or heard
of something like that . . . It's horrible." "Yes, truly horrible
and humiliating," and as proof I reached my hands toward
him so he could smell them. "Blech," he said, and held back
from vomiting. Then he left, but returned right after to give
me his book, he explained where his room was and asked if

I was free that evening for a walk through the forest. I told him yes and we agreed to meet at five at the castle entrance.

I was about to look at Hugo's book when the old servant came and gave me a note from Anibal in which he told me that he didn't have time to educate the wild girl and that he was leaving her in my charge, that he expected to see results soon. And so I went down, untied the girl, and brought her up to my room.

The first thing I noticed was that under the grime, which made it look like she had dark skin, she was very pale, and so I took her to the bathroom. She was very gentle and let me clean her with a brush. I dried her and gave her one of my shirts, which fitted her like a dress. We returned to my room and I sat her on my nightstand. The fingers on her hands were very thick, especially the thumbs, perhaps from using them so much to climb trees. She had green eyes, small and clear, and dark-brown hair. She was a pretty child, about ten or eleven years old. She didn't talk or make any noise, and almost didn't move. She seemed like a doll. And yet, when I took out the salami and offered it to her, she swiftly took it out of my hands and ate it in big bites. It was then that I realized I was also hungry, that I felt a hunger like that of a . . . Then I told her, making a kind face and gesturing a lot with my hands, that I was going to look for food, to wait for me. She seemed to understand. I went down, went into the dining room, and through what seemed to be the kitchen door. It was the kitchen, and nobody was there. From the refrigerator, which was full of all types of food, I grabbed some prosciutto sandwiches and cheese and a bottle of juice and went up to my room. The girl was no longer there; I looked through the window and saw her running toward the forest. She ran in a very particular way: a little hunched over, she placed one foot in front of the other very quickly; she seemed to glide across the grass. I was about to go out and look for her, but it seemed pointless to me. What could I teach her? Besides, I was more worried about having to kill Anibal. The situation had me a little nervous: once, I had killed a slave, but it had been in self-defense. In any case, I felt that there wasn't any danger, since nobody would come out to defend Anibal: not Hugo, nor the servants, nor Ninive. The only one who could defend him was me. And then I noticed how strange it was that there were no guards in the castle.

CHAPTER 6

I ATE THE sandwiches while looking at the book. It was a very boring book about death and funerary rites. Then I went down and met up with Hugo, who told me: "That book is good." "What book?" I asked. "Yours." "Ah, but it's not mine, it was already there." He looked at me weird: "What's wrong? You're ashamed?" "No, not at all." "Ah, because I like it." "What are you trying to say?" He didn't respond. We walked a little and, when we entered the forest, Hugo pushed me against a tree and started kissing my neck. Trying to push him off I noticed that he was stronger than me. "Stop it," I shouted. "Okay, calm down," he said, relaxing his grip on me. "Stop fucking around!" I shouted again. "With what?" "With the homosexual positions!" "Fine, okay, I thought we could have fun." "I don't find it fun." "Okay, okay, forget it. Anyway I've already told you I like women. It's just that this book . . ." "What?" "I don't know, it makes you want to try everything." "It didn't make me feel like doing anything when I saw it." "Fine, it could be me, I don't know, doesn't matter." "Fine, but leave me the fuck alone." "Perfect, understood."

There was a silence and then Hugo spoke: "Ninive told me you're thinking about killing Anibal." "What!?" I shouted. "What? It's a lie?" I stayed silent. "Look," he said, "if you need help, tell me. I don't want to do the work he's made you do; I'm capable of any job, but I have a limit and that's too disgusting. And besides, I think it's the moment for us to start breaking the chains of slavery." "Which chains?" "I think we could decide what to do with our lives." "Perhaps . . ." "But then, are you going to kill him?" "I guess so." "Ninive is really enthusiastic about the idea. She told me every detail about what Anibal does to her . . . It's horrible . . ." "She told you what he does to her?" "Yes, why? You don't know?" "No, yes, of course I know, but I thought that she was ashamed of talking about it." "Yes, for good reason. But we were chatting for some time." "Ah, I see." "Ninive told me that if you didn't plan on killing him, I could do it. I don't mind doing it, but if you want revenge for the jobs that he forced you to do, better that you do it; besides, I think that she wants you to do it." "Yes, *I* will do it." "Fine by me, better, it's not fun killing people." We walked a while longer and returned to the castle. By the door was Ninive, who greeted each of us with a kiss. "So?" she asked. "*I* will do it," I said with an angry expression. "Perfect. When? Today?" she asked with a very feminine and indescribable gesture, and I got scared and, feigning surprise, said: "Today?" "Yes, what's the problem?" "Fine, today," I replied and went up to my room, very agitated, angry, and nervous. I threw myself on my bed for a while; then I got up and decided to go to Ninive's room to ask her why she had told Hugo what Anibal did to her, and not me. I arrived and, when I was about to knock on the door, I heard Hugo's voice.

I almost left, but instead I banged on the door, and Ninive opened it. "Come in, Hugo and I were chatting just now." "Yeah?" "Yeah." "Hello," Hugo said, "I was just about to go. Bye, Nini." "Bye, Hughug." When Hugo left I asked Ninive what that stuff about "Hughug" and "Nini" was all about, why she had told him those things and not me, if they were lovers or what, etc. She laughed and told me not to be silly: "I'm only interested in you. But with Hugo one can have a nice chat: as big and rough as he is, he knows how to listen with a lot of delicacy." "And I don't?" "Well, you're more con-voluted, every idea brings you to another, and another, etc. Hugo has a more simple way of thinking, more linear . . ." "Ah." Then she grabbed my hands, looked me in the eyes and added: "Besides, I don't want your image of me to become tainted with the images of the horrible things Anibal does to me." And she gave me a kiss on the mouth and asked me to please kill Anibal. I told her yes and left feeling joyful.

CHAPTER 7

IN MY ROOM, I spent some time thinking about how I would kill Anibal, and I arrived at the conclusion that it would be best to use the knife I had for the salami. It was a very lovely knife, quite big and sharp, with a wooden handle and an interesting shape, soft and animal-like. While I thought about Anibal's death, I began to absentmindedly write my name with the knife on the nightstand. When I saw it, I noticed that this new engraving on the nightstand had been carved on top of the older one, in such a way that it was impossible to read my name. "Better," I said out loud, and stood, jumped a little while shaking the knife, and looked out the window. It was night already. I didn't feel fear or anything like it: Anibal's death, for me, was already a fact. And I was about to go out looking for him when all of a sudden the castle's front door opened and out came Anibal, who looked upward and saw me with the knife in my hand. "What are you doing there with a knife?" he shouted at me. "I'm eating salami," I replied without getting nervous. "Careful, you could drop it and hurt someone." "Yes, sorry," I replied, and threw it on the bed. He continued speaking: "I'm waiting for my son, who's about to arrive." "Your son! He's coming today?" I asked, trying to sound relaxed. "I don't know, I think so, but maybe not." I pulled myself inside and sat on the bed. With his son present, killing Anibal would be more difficult, and I didn't want to kill them both; at the same time, I had promised Ninive that I would do it. On the other hand, if I killed Anibal right now and his son arrived later, things could become complicated. All of a sudden I heard the sound of engines. I went to the window and saw a car and motorcycles coming to a halt. A man got out of the car, without a doubt it was Anibal's son, accompanied by a beautiful woman and three children under five. Anibal shouted with joy and the children ran to him; "Grandpa, Grandpa," they shouted; they were a girl and two boys. Then, they all embraced and entered the castle. The men on the motorcycles stayed outside smoking cigarettes and chatting among themselves; there were five of them and they seemed to be guards.

All of this disturbed me: the idea of family, the children, the guards. To kill Anibal, something so simple before, suddenly seemed impossible. And then I heard shrieking and saw Hugo in the distance returning from the forest and dragging what looked to be the wild girl by the hair. When he arrived at the castle door he looked at me and raised an arm in celebration of his victory. The girl was mutely shaking. "Where do I put her?" he asked me. "I don't know . . . at the back of the castle, next to the kitchen door, there's a cage, you can put her there." Then I saw him leave and I realized that I would have preferred for the girl to stay in the forest, because I felt pity, and also because it annoyed me to have to educate her, and because I didn't feel I could teach her anything.

I exited the castle. The bikers were at the door. I waved to them and they waved back. "How's it going?" I said. "Just here, protecting the boss," one of them replied. "That's good," I said, and circled the castle. By the kitchen door, in the cage, the girl was sleeping. Hugo had locked her in and furthermore had tied one of her legs to a bar. Her leg was swollen from the pressure of the rope. It seemed excessive, so I untied her, and when I did, without moving she opened her eyes a little and looked at me like she was grateful; then, for some reason, I unhooked the cage door: if she wanted to, let her escape. I entered the kitchen to look for something to eat and ran into Ninive, the old servant, the young servant, and Hugo. "What are you all doing here?" I asked them, and Ninive told me: "Shh." They were glued to the door, listening to what Anibal and his son were saying in the dining room. The son was telling him that he should have guards, that it wasn't safe to be alone, without protection, so far from all the other houses, and Anibal replied that he didn't like guards, that he had a good relationship with the people in his castle and all of them would protect him if necessary. In the kitchen everyone laughed under their breath; Hugo said: "Yes, of course, except that we're going to kill you," and everyone laughed again. I didn't find it funny; quite the opposite, it made me anxious. "You're killing him today?" the young servant asked me while she caressed Hugo under his pants. "What?" I replied. "You're not killing him?" asked Ninive, as if she was angry. "Yes, but not today." "Why?" Hugo asked me, carefree. "I don't know, he's with his entire family," I said. "And what's that got to do with anything?" asked Ninive. "I'll kill him tomorrow," I said. There was a silence and then we heard Anibal's son, who was saying: "Slavery is humiliating. We shouldn't tolerate it anymore." And Anibal replied: "It's intolerable, I agree. But you know I support the legal path." And the son, a little agitated, replied: "No! There is no legal path! Slavery should end right now." "What? They want to abolish slavery?" I asked, surprised, and everyone laughed. "They're speaking of metaphorical slavery. They consider themselves slaves of the central power," Ninive explained to me. "Central power?" I asked again. "Yes," answered the young servant while she kissed Hugo's neck, "the central power is responsible for determining the laws, like for example income taxes, etc." The children started squealing and Anibal shouted: "Food!" and the old servant entered the dining room with a pot. Then we left through the kitchen door and Hugo, when he saw that the wild girl had escaped, started saying: "No, no, no," and threw himself on the floor, crying. "What's wrong?" I asked him, and the young servant replied: "Anibal told Hugo that he would destroy his face with a whip if he didn't bring back the girl." "Really?" asked Ninive. "Yes," replied Hugo crying, and looking at me, he said, "You saw that I brought her back." "Yes, yes," I replied, "but don't worry, we'll trap her." "Now? At night? It's very dangerous," said the young servant. "Why?" I asked. "Because the forest is full of wild animals," replied Ninive. "Animals who feed on humans," added the old servant. And Hugo concluded: "I'm doomed." Then Ninive told me: "You have to kill him today: if not for me, at least do it for Hugo." And I told Hugo: "Hugo, we could kill him between the two of us." But since Hugo was crying so much that he couldn't respond, the young servant told me, while caressing his left ear with one finger: "Hugo's depressed, he won't be able to do anything today, only sleep and cry. Luckily I'm here to console him." And Ninive told me: "Besides, you said that you would do it, and now we all have it set in our minds that you will." I wanted to ask why everyone should depend on me, but didn't, and remained standing next to the empty cage watching them all go. In the distance, I heard Hugo say: "This miserable life . . ."

CHAPTER 8

I RETURNED TO the castle. At the front door, the bikers had set up a portable table and were playing cards. "All good?" I asked. They didn't respond. I was about to enter the castle, but instead I went out in the direction of the forest: I wanted to distance myself for a while from the mess that had happened. I went around in circles for a long time, very agitated, thinking about Anibal, about Hugo, about Ninive, about the girl . . . I knew I couldn't kill Anibal that night. That stuff about the son visiting could be an excuse, but in any case, what mattered was that I didn't feel like it. I had to accept that Ninive would see me as a coward. I also felt bad for Hugo, but why didn't he kill him? And so, winding myself around my thoughts, little by little and without realizing it, I wandered into the deepest, densest, and darkest part of the forest, and got lost. But I only realized I was lost when I heard a roar; and since the roar sounded closer each time, I got scared. Instinctively, I climbed a tree, and from up above I saw an animal similar to a bear approach. I kept still. The animal circled a few times sniffing around and lay down at the foot of my tree. I had found a hole between two branches that turned out to be very comfortable, and despite the fear I felt, I fell asleep, trying not to move. I don't know how much later I woke up with a start, perhaps because of a bite from some insect. My sudden movement woke the animal, who then noticed me and began to growl. Despite the darkness I could see that it was a terrifying creature, much more terrifying than a bear, or at least more terrifying than the image I had of a bear, because I had never seen one up so close. I tried climbing higher, but it was impossible, and when it saw me trying to escape, the creature started to hit the tree, which was thick, with such force that I thought it would knock it down. Instead of climbing, then, I clung to a branch and started to shout at the bear not to harm me, but that, for some reason, agitated it further, and its agitation agitated me and made me shout at it more forcibly. The situation was very dramatic, and what I began to think in that moment, in between shakings, shouts, and roars, was the following: I didn't want to kill Anibal and now I would die. I also sensed something very obvious, yet revelatory to me, because I felt like a man who . . . Meanwhile, the bear kept hitting the tree trunk, which was already a little inclined, with its body, its arms, and its head, and I had stopped shouting: I just clung there and provided a counterweight to delay the final fall. And then, just as I was thinking about the possibility of fighting with the bear body to body, that is, of measuring my strength against it despite the nonexistent possibilities of winning, we heard, both the bear and I, a little, very high-pitched shout. And when we both looked, we saw the same thing: some four yards away, the wild girl was threatening it with a stick.

And I'm sure that had the general conditions been different, both the bear and I would have laughed, and everything would have ended in the best possible way. What happened, instead, was that the bear paused and then began to growl at the girl, who not only didn't flinch but began to shake her weapon so that one could see there were cords, with rocks at the ends, attached to the stick. That's to say, the weapon the girl had was a combination of a stick and a *boleadora*. That agitated the bear, who stood on its hind legs and let out a horrible roar, then the girl made a very quick move forward, like she was gliding, made a precise maneuver with her stick, and backed away just as quickly, as we heard a noise like broken glass, and bloody shards of teeth started falling out of the bear's mouth. The bear fell almost to its knees, roaring, and then stood up and, when it saw the girl spinning the stick, took a jump toward her, but the girl, instead of running away, threw her weapon at the bear: the cords snagged the animal in midair and it fell heavily to the ground. Then the girl climbed on top of it and nailed the other side of the stick, which was sharp, into its throat. The gurgle of blood was heard, and the bear died. Scared and in shock, I had no intention to climb down, until the girl made some gestures with her hands that led me to understand her aim was not to kill me as well, on the contrary, she had just saved my life, probably as a reward for having left the door of her cage open.

As soon as I climbed down the tree, the girl gave me some roots she was carrying in some sort of leather pouch that hung from a rope tied around her waist. Apart from the rope and the pouch, she was completely naked. I ate the roots without thinking twice, and by the time the girl began to open the bear's stomach with a little wooden knife, I was already softly hallucinating. We ate the bear, raw, in a ritual that consisted in spinning around and running a bit each time we took out a new organ; afterward we fell asleep on the spot. I woke up with the morning light, still hallucinating and covered in dried blood. The girl wasn't there, but then she suddenly appeared and took me to a nearby stream. Before going into the water, we ate some more roots, and I believe it was at that moment that my brain lost all judgment, memory, and order.

I spent many days in the forest with the girl; in that time, I learned to recognize the different types of roots by their distinct effects, shapes, and modes of consumption; to hunt animals big and small and eat them in different ways, always raw; to converse with insects and plants and to find sources of water. Always in silence, because the girl didn't speak and didn't know how to laugh. She also taught me how to glide like her: one foot in front of the other, almost without lifting them off the ground, very quickly. It was the best way of closing in on the animals we wanted to eat. And one day, in a hallucinatory state, I got lost. I was alone for many long hours, searching unsuccessfully for the girl and eating different roots that drove me crazy, until, perhaps unintentionally, I arrived at a treeless hill, and from that hill I saw the castle illuminated by the sun, and I understood, or came to believe, that she had hidden from me because she wanted me to return to my place, which was the castle. And then, feeling very agitated, I ate the wrong root or took too high a dose and set off running in no particular direction with my head full of images of Anibal and Ninive and the jobs that Anibal had made me do, and although I wasn't heading in any particular direction, all of a sudden, I found myself some two hundred yards from the door of the castle and saw Anibal, who signaled to me and shouted across the distance, holding a whip in his hand. I don't know how, but suddenly I felt a lashing on my shoulder and noticed I was only six feet from Anibal. When I saw the wound, which seemed enormous to me, I lunged at him with animalistic fury, and we rolled around for some time until I somehow managed to push the whip's handle into his left eye; this made him scream and softened him up a bit, so then I quickly took the handle out of his eye socket and, using both hands, pressed it against his throat until he was motionless, dead. The commotion of Anibal's screaming had brought out Ninive, Hugo, and the young servant. When I got to my feet, dirty, wild, and covered in bloodstains, Hugo and the young servant stood back, but Ninive came up to me, kissed me on the mouth, and told me, in a victorious tone: "Now you're the king!" I replied that I was very tired, and then she took me to my room and left me sleeping in my bed.

CHAPTER 9

WHEN I WOKE up, just the next day, the first thing I saw was breakfast on the nightstand. I reached for the kettle and noticed it was warm. I got up and opened the window. It was a pleasant day, neither hot nor cold, and the port bustled with activity. In the distance, at the border between sky and sea, the Navy trained its sailors to fire cannons. The way some of the sounds echoed in my head reminded me that I was under the influence of some root. But the effect was fading. I felt good, and didn't remember what I had been up to until I saw my hands; then I ran out to shower.

Once clean, I started drinking the tea, which had by now become tepid, and ate some bread, which had hardened a bit. In that moment, all the previous days in the forest and the death of Anibal seemed like a dream to me, and just when I was beginning to suspect that it had truly been a dream, two things happened at the same time: first, I saw the whip mark on my arm and noticed that it was very superficial; second, Ninive opened the door, shouted "Our king!" and ran toward me and embraced me. "What's that about a *king*?"

I asked. "Well, now that Anibal is dead and buried . . ." "They buried him? Already?" "Yes, yes, I think so. For some reason, this morning he already appeared to be swollen with worms. Hugo buried him in the forest." "In the forest?" "Yes, that's what he said, why?" "Nothing, no reason." We remained silent, and then I once more asked: "What's that about a *king*?" "Oh, I don't know, but it's fun, right?" "Yes . . ." There was another silence, and then Ninive, in a silly voice, asked: "And would I be the queen?" There I cheered up and told her: "Of course." "Really?" she insisted. "Yes, yes, of course!" I said, more effusively this time. Then, quite content, she jumped on me and we got into bed and gave freedom to our more animal instincts.

Later, Ninive asked me what I had done in those days; and I replied, trying to make myself mysterious, that I had been communing with nature, gathering strength for what I must do. When we went down to the castle entrance, the old servant, the young servant, and Hugo were there, in front of a table full of delicious food. "We prepared it for you," said the young servant, and then I looked at Hugo and was horrified: his face was covered in welts. "No!" I said. "Yes, it's what Anibal had promised. All the same, I don't care anymore, because I got my revenge: before burying him I destroyed the body so that . . ." "Oh, okay," I replied. Then the young servant told me that since my departure Anibal had gone completely insane with the whip, and she lifted her skirt and showed me her behind and her legs, which were injured, but not gravely so. "Me too," said the old servant, and showed me her arms and shoulders, also injured by the whip. "And he didn't do anything to you?" I asked Ninive, because I hadn't seen injuries on her body. "Yes, he did the same that he always did to me, but with more cruelty." "Oh, no!" exclaimed Hugo, the young servant, and the old servant in chorus, a little theatrically. I wanted to ask Ninive what it was that Anibal had done to her, but I imagined her answer and didn't. Hugo then insisted: "This banquet is in your honor." "Thanks," I replied. "Well, let's sit down," said Ninive. "And where are the kids?" asked the young servant. "Ah, of course," said Hugo, and whistled, and two kids around sixteen years old appeared, very pitiful and thin. I asked who they were, and Ninive replied that they were two new slaves whom Anibal had acquired for a pittance. Since the kids were very frightened, I told them to calm down, that we were all free now, and that no one would hit them or treat them badly, and as if to show them my authority, I shouted, "Let's eat at once, I'm famished!" and we sat down to eat.

When we finished, I went up to my room. I looked out the window and saw the sunset. Activity on the port was winding down. A man washed an almost-empty cage of slaves with a hose. Ninive knocked on the door and entered. She told me, again, that I was the king and that to her anything I did would be okay, and we were passionately kissing when someone knocked on the door. "Yes?" I asked. It was the new teens, who wanted to leave. "And go where?" I asked. "The city," one replied. "Which city?" I asked. "No, no, town," corrected the other. "Ah, you want to go to the town?" I said in a reflective tone. "Yes," they replied. "Why? What's there?" I asked. "Everyone and everything is there, we want to live there, it's the best place for us, with a lot of opportunities," they replied excitedly. "Okay, go . . ." I told them, and so they thanked me and left. I wanted to go back to kissing Ninive, but she had fallen asleep in bed in a very weird position. Later, when she woke up, she asked if she could move into my room because hers was scarred by the memories of the things Anibal had done to her. I told her I didn't mind, but that the bed wasn't big enough. She told me she didn't mind, that we could bring in Anibal's bed, which was enormous and super comfortable. I repressed the urge to ask any questions and told her it seemed like a good idea.

Anibal's room was very close to mine. It was, in fact, identical to mine, although a little bigger and with a private bathroom. It, too, faced the front of the castle, and the view was very similar, with a slight difference in angle. "And what if we moved in here?" I asked her. She stood there thinking awhile and then told me no, she didn't think it was a good idea. So then, with the help of Hugo and the two servants we disassembled the bed and rebuilt it in my room. Hugo asked for my previous bed, and I gave it to him.

At night, during dinner, Hugo told me about a plan that had occurred to him: to go buy more slaves, emancipate them, train them, and invade Anibal's son's castle to free the slaves who were there, of which there were surely many. We discussed the details and arrived at the idea that, given that Anibal's son, from what he had said, must have, in addition to the bikers, many guards, we would need at least fifty slaves. "Could we buy that many? Where did Anibal keep the money?" I asked. The young servant said that she knew there was a safe in the library, which we could try to open. We went there and she showed us a little door behind some books. Hugo threw the shelving down and we saw that the safe was quite secure. "Let me do it, I know something about this," he said, and so we gave him some room and let him work with his ear up against the mechanism. Ninive said that she was going to the bathroom, and the old servant left because she was sleepy. So I asked the young servant her name. "Idomenea," she replied. "Ah, what a pretty name." "Thanks. And yet, no one uses it, they call me whatever: Chufa, Wolf, Blackie, Fonfi . . ." "Ah, well, I'll use Idomenea," I said, and she smiled, told me thanks, and surprisingly, perhaps taking advantage of Hugo's back being to us, placed her hand inside my shirt and began to caress my chest and stomach. I took her hand out, and then, as if it were nothing, she went to Hugo's side and started caressing his hair and neck. Ninive came back with some chocolates. "They were in Anibal's room," she said. While we ate the chocolates, Ninive and I chatted and watched Hugo work and Idomenea caress him all over. "That woman is unbelievable," Ninive whispered in my ear. "Right?" I said. "Yes, yes. Sometimes she starts caressing me and I have to remove her hand," she replied. I laughed. Suddenly we heard a click and a shout of joy from Hugo. We approached him, congratulated him, and immediately saw that there wasn't that much money. We counted it and confirmed that it was enough to buy anywhere from thirty to thirty-five slaves. "It'll suffice," said Hugo. And then I saw that one of the wounds on his face was festering and told him so. "Yes, it's infected, but it doesn't matter, it'll heal," he said, and we left. Idomenea and Ninive went to their rooms, and Hugo and I went out to the castle door to smoke some cigars we'd found in the library. "The stars are lovely, aren't they?" Hugo said. I agreed, and said this meant that the next day many ships with many slaves would arrive and that we should go early to get a good bargain. At that moment, Hugo became troubled and looked off to one side; when I asked him what was wrong, he told me that he wanted to go alone. "Why?" I asked. "You're the king of the castle. Let me do something." A little annoyed, I told him it was fine, and then threw my cigar on the floor, crushed it with my foot, and went to bed.

Chapter 10

The next day, I woke up and saw breakfast on the nightstand. I worked out that the person who left it was the old servant, because Ninive was still sleeping and Idomenea must be with Hugo. I reached for the kettle and noticed it was warm. I got up and opened the window. Five slaves were shooting from a platform full of slaves and were moving slowly along the road to the castle. Hugo was walking with his hands in his pockets, whistling. I dressed quickly, went down, ran a few minutes until reaching them, and approached Hugo. "What's wrong with you? Why are you making the slaves work?" "They're slaves, we'll liberate them after," replied Hugo. "No, they're not slaves. They have to arrive free at the castle," I told him, and ordered the ones carrying the cage to lower it. "No!" Hugo told me, but I looked at him harshly, walked up to the cage, and opened it. "Get out, please, you're free," I said, and little by little, without understanding much, the slaves started exiting the cage. They were dirty and tired. "How many are there?" I asked Hugo. "Forty-five," he replied. "Really? That's good." When they all left, I asked them to listen to me, and told them that they were free and that together we would liberate others. They didn't seem to understand, so I pointed to the castle and told them to walk toward it. "What do we do with the cage?" asked one of the slaves who had been carrying it. "Leave it there, we don't need it anymore," I replied.

When we got to the castle, Hugo asked them to arrange themselves. "How?" asked one. "In a line, how else?" replied Hugo harshly. Then he counted them, got close to me, and whispered in my ear, annoyed and as if accusing me: "There are eight missing, they must have escaped." "Doesn't matter," I replied, "those were the worst." "No," he said, "there was a very muscular one." "In any case . . . These things happen," I said trying not to care. Hugo ran up to the house, came out with a hose, which he connected to a faucet in the garden, and violently blasted the slaves, who whimpered a bit. Then he asked me where we would make them sleep. I said that I didn't know, that we would see. It seemed appropriate to tell them something at that moment, and I told them what came out: that the voice of freedom was in our hearts and that it was our objective to make it shout louder and louder, and that it was better to be dead than a slave. There was a silence, and so, feeling uncomfortable, I decided to shout this last part as a slogan: "Better dead than slaves!" I shouted again, this time looking at Hugo so he could repeat it with me. Hugo and I repeated it, and one or two slaves also livened up. By the fifth time, most of them were with us. By the tenth, we all passionately shouted: "Better dead than slaves!"

Chapter 11

I ENTERED THE castle and, with Ninive's help, looked for the room full of hunting trophies that I'd once seen. As I'd assumed, it also had a wide assortment of weapons: for some reason, there were ten rifles; there was also the red rifle, which I decided to grab for myself for symbolic reasons and upon doing so I understood why Anibal had preferred to use this one the time we went hunting; there were many handguns and many knives, and other weapons, strange and inexplicable. We gathered everything in a cart Ninive had found and took it to the garden. Hugo was there attempting to line up the slaves, who weren't listening to him; when they saw me, however, they became happy and ordered themselves in a kind of row. "Better dead than slaves!" I shouted, and they repeated after me with enthusiasm. I noticed that they now realized they were free and saw how their mood and even posture had changed. I explained that we had weapons and that Hugo, who would be their captain moving forward, would be responsible for seeing who would use which, according to his merits and individual talents. I also explained that my rifle, red in color, symbolized the bloodshed of thousands of slaves throughout History, and that this blood, in my rifle, would fire upon the oppressor pigs. "Better dead than slaves! Die oppressor pigs!" they shouted. Then I explained into Hugo's ear that I still hadn't found more than a small box of bullets for the rifles, but that he needn't worry because I knew that Anibal had thousands; that in any case he should start making formations, movements, whatever. Probably happy just to have the title of captain, he told me to trust in him, everything would turn out fine, and that if we didn't find ammunition we could buy it. "With what money?" I asked. "Uh," he said. So I told him not to worry and, in a loud voice, exclaimed: "Onward, Captain Hugo."

When I entered the castle, Ninive, who had been watching me, embraced me and said that, even though she'd believed in me from the beginning, she never would have imagined I'd be such a good king and give such good and effective speeches. I told her she was a perfect queen, and that she was lovelier than ever. That last part was true: her features had softened and her posture was much more distinguished. Then I told her I was worried about the bullets and asked if she could look for them with the help of the other two women. "Don't worry," she said. Then I went for a stroll through the forest. I hoped to see the wild girl, but there was no trace to lead me to her. I looked at plants and identified some roots. And suddenly I saw the plant whose roots I'd eaten before killing Anibal. "Let's see . . ." I said out loud, and pulled up the root, sitting on the ground to look it over, and I realized that the one I'd eaten in the forest wasn't the one I'd thought it was, but another, which was almost unknown to me, though it was very similar to one I did know, and I stowed it away in my pocket without knowing what for. A few minutes later, I was watching a bird with a worm in its beak while I thought worriedly about the lack of bullets, and then it hit me: before the battle, the warriors would eat the root.

When I returned, Ninive told me they'd looked everywhere, but with no success, save for another small box of bullets that would only work in the handguns. "It's not much . . . ," I said. I counted the bullets we had: barely more than two for each rifle and one for each handgun. So I told her about my idea and explained that we should gather lots of roots; I showed her the plant and she told me that she, Idomenea, and the old servant would go together to gather some . . . "What's it called?" she asked. "I don't know . . . let's call it *wild girl*." Ninive smiled: "How lovely, *wild girl*." I asked her where the other two women were, and she told me they were in the kitchen, preparing food for the troop. "And you?" I asked. "Not me, I'm the queen." "Ninive," I said: "we must all do our part." Then she, with a proud attitude, went to the kitchen. I followed her, congratulated the women for their work, and grabbed a sandwich to eat. With the sandwich in hand, I dedicated myself to finding a place in the castle where I could put up the troop. There wasn't anything that big, and it didn't seem right to put them far away from us, and so I decided that they would sleep in groups of five in the empty rooms that were to be found all over.

That day, time went by very quickly: we were constantly busy with organizing everything for the troop: food, beds, etc. At night, while we ate something in my room, Hugo told me that he was satisfied with the way training had gone and that it seemed to him they would be ready in two days to go to the castle. When I told him we hadn't found a sufficient quantity of bullets, he replied that, foreseeing this possibility, an idea had occurred to him: "We can sell three or four of the sick ones and use that money to buy bullets." I spoke to him firmly: "Hugo, there's something you don't understand: they're not slaves, we can't sell them." "But they are, we bought them and . . ." I raised my voice: "*But* nothing. Besides, I have a better idea." I then explained the thing about the roots, which at first didn't convince him. "It's better than bullets," I told him, "they provoke a destructive fury." "A destructive fury? Fine, there doesn't seem to be any other option." "No, at least I can't think of one." "No, me neither."

Suddenly, we heard a lot of noise and voices: it was the slaves settling in. They seemed happy. So then I talked to Hugo about my project of burning down all the places where Anibal had made me work. "I need to do it to forget them," I explained, and immediately images appeared in my mind of the humiliation to which I had been subjected. "No one, never, has been subjected to something like this," Hugo told me, and recommended I do it after he left with the troop, so as not to cause chaos. "What? I'm going too, Hugo," I said in surprise. "No, I thought about it and it doesn't seem like a good idea. Someone has to stay here, in this conquered castle. We can't abandon it. You, the king, should stay with five soldiers. And with the car, so you can visit me." "And then what?" "Well, it seems to me that once we conquer that other castle, which must be enormous, I could stay there and arm another group with another captain to conquer another castle, I don't know . . ." "You want to keep conquering castles?"

"Well . . . Yes, I suppose I do. If not, then what?" "I haven't thought about it . . ." We both remained silent. At first I was shocked, but later I had to admit that it was a quite a good plan, and so I told him it was good, we would do just that.

Chapter 12

I woke up the next day and saw breakfast on the nightstand. I reached for the kettle and noticed it was warm. Ninive was sleeping. I got up and opened the window. It was a pleasant day, neither hot nor cold, and below, in the garden, Hugo passionately trained the troop: he made them run, throw themselves on the ground, aim with the rifles and handguns, jump over some bundles with knives between their teeth. Separately, a group of five soldiers trained with the strange weaponry; somehow, they appeared to master it and gave off a dangerous impression. I woke Ninive up, offered her a cup of tea, and asked her not to forget to gather the roots. "The *wild girls*," she said with a smile and a sleepy voice, her eyes still half-closed. "Yes, the *wild girls*," I replied, seriously, and gave her a kiss.

The day passed very quickly. In the evening, before sunset, the three women returned from the forest with an enormous basket full of roots. "Great," I said. And then Ninive explained that in the beginning they couldn't find any, but that at a certain moment they saw the wild girl and started following her because it seemed like that was what she wanted them to do, and so they arrived at a spot full of these plants. "Great, that girl is . . ." I showed Hugo the roots. "How lovely," he said. And it was true, the roots were very lovely: red, furry, and slimy, soft and fleshy on the outside, but with a very thin core, like a bone you could feel when you squeezed them; they seemed to be from another planet, and possibly they were. We washed them and left them to dry on a table at the castle entrance. Hugo told me the troop was ready, that the following morning they would head off to conquer the castle. "Great," I said, and then something occurred to me and, feeling panicked, I asked him: "Do you know where it is, how to get there?" Hugo went pale. Without saying anything, we left to find Ninive and asked her, but she didn't know either. Neither did Idomenea, and so we went to find the old servant. She thought she knew, although she wasn't very sure; she had gone once, years ago, when the castle belonged to . . . "But how do you get there?" asked Hugo. "Well," she said, "it's that way," and she pointed, with a trembling hand, in the direction opposite the port. "The town is that way," I said. "Yes, the town," she said. "No, but we're looking for the castle belonging to . . ." "Yes, yes, it's before the town." "Where?" "I don't know, many years have passed, I used to go looking for . . ." "Please," we said, and then she believed she remembered there was a map in the library. We ran to the library and spent hours searching through everything. Every now and then, a ticked-off Hugo would rip a book apart, to let off steam, usually a very old one; at times even a manuscript made of parchment or papyrus. At some point, Hugo called to me, "Look at this!"

Hidden among the books, there were some bottles containing very strange, semi-human fetuses. We left them to one side, taken aback, and kept searching for the map for an hour, but without any success. Then I got an idea: to see if there were any tracks left from the motorcycles. Hugo loved this idea, and told me that I wasn't king for nothing. "I'm the king because I killed Anibal," I told him. "Yes, yes, but on top of that you have that head which . . ." We ran out to the garden. It was already a little dark; all the same, after a while, we were able to see the motorcycle tracks and followed them a few yards. At times they stopped, but Hugo said what we had was enough. "Nothing will stop us!" he shouted, and we headed toward the dining room, where we dined with our women and got a little drunk.

At night, lying with Ninive, I heard men moaning from pleasure. "What's that?" I asked, and Ninive laughed. "What's so funny?" I asked her. "I don't know . . . you didn't hear them last night?" "No . . . ," I said, and fell silent, then she told me that she believed she'd seen one of the soldiers with the book on sexual positions. "Really?" I asked. "Yes, I think so." I lay there thinking, and then I said: "You know what? Sometimes I get the feeling that these new liberated slaves don't understand what happened to them, and as such can't see themselves as free, but also not as slaves, and for the time being they're only soldiers, which is no more than a transitory role. I don't know how this will evolve. What will they be afterward?" Ninive said that I shouldn't think about these things, that there would be time, but I disagreed and said that this *was* the time, because afterward, how would they stop being soldiers? They'll want to turn this role into an identity, and then they'd want to keep fighting even after the enemy was extinguished. "The enemy is never extinguished," she told me, and I lay in bed reflecting on that until I fell asleep.

CHAPTER 13

THE FOLLOWING MORNING, I woke up and saw breakfast on the nightstand. Ninive was sleeping with her mouth open. I went to the window and opened it. Outside, it was a little cold, but pleasant, and below, in the garden, the troop was lined up, and Hugo inspected each soldier with authority. I shouted a hello, and he sent one back; then they all looked at me, and I shouted: "Better dead than slaves!" And below they all answered: "Die oppressor pigs!" When I turned around, Ninive had woken up. She seemed preoccupied. "Ninive, what's wrong?" I asked her. "I don't know, I had a bad dream." "Oh yeah? About what?" "I don't remember, but it was ugly. Something happened to us, to you and me, and we had to escape." "Escape from where?" "I don't know, I don't remember." "Well, don't worry," I told her, and poured her a cup of tea.

Afterward, I went down and gave a speech to the troop. I told them a lot of things, and ended with the following idea: "Even if I am born a slave and a master raises and feeds me, and even if my parents and grandparents were or are slaves, even in that case I'm free from the moment I decide to be, because the moment in which I decide is the moment in which I become conscious of the difference between slavery and freedom, and that consciousness of the difference is freedom itself, and the action which takes me toward actual freedom is only one step away from that decision. But without this decision, there's nothing." Then there was an uncomfortable silence. I realized no one had understood anything, and Hugo, to remedy this, shouted: "Better dead than slaves. Die oppressor pigs!" And they all repeated this, as did I. Then Hugo took me aside and asked me not to say things like that again. "Why? They're important things." "Yes," he replied, "that's true, but they don't understand them, and that makes them insecure, and there's nothing worse than an insecure soldier." "Fine," I said, "but after the battle I'm going to the castle to make them understand the idea." "Okay, there'll be time. Anyway, I'm not sure I agree: perhaps it's the reverse," he replied. "The reverse, how?" "Well, perhaps consciousness arrives after actual freedom." "Ah, perhaps . . . But I don't think so," I said. "Okay, we'll see. Because these ones don't have consciousness, but they do have freedom, and if everything goes well, consciousness will appear on its own." And after saying this, Hugo returned to the troop and shouted at them that the battle they would engage in would be decisive, that they would liberate many enslaved brothers and sisters and that this liberation would lead to others, etc. Later I took Hugo aside again and asked him to be careful with the roots, to not give them too much because it could be dangerous; that it would be best for them to eat them right before attacking the castle, because I thought the effect was brief, and then

I considered, although I didn't say anything, that it had been dumb not to do any tests on the effects beforehand. Hugo told me not to worry and said he would send me a messenger with news of a victory. Then he shouted, "Calambra!" and a soldier approached, very short and with a face that made one think of . . . and who I didn't like at all. "This is Calambra!" said Hugo, "my right-hand man." "It's an honor," Calambra told me, "you're our role model." "Well, thanks," I replied, and he insisted: "We all want to be like you." "Okay, okay," I said, and gave him a little push to make him go away.

Immediately after, the troop formed and started to march behind Hugo; at Hugo's side, to my surprise, was Idomenea, and ahead of Hugo, hunched over, was Calambra, who was looking for traces of the motorcycles and led the way. At the door of the castle, Ninive and the old servant chatted with the five soldiers who were staying with us. I went over to them and told them everything would be fine. "Surely," said one of the soldiers, who was named Justino and was very tall and much older than the other four, who had strange names and were practically indistinguishable one from the other. I told them that after lunch, later in the day, we had a job to do, which was to burn down the facilities where the owner of the castle had made me suffer the unbearable humiliations that had led me to seek freedom, which ended in their liberation, and that therefore burning down that place would be a symbol to all. "In the meantime," I told them, "please go to the library and bury the jars with fetuses that you will find there."

CHAPTER 14

I HAD BREAKFAST with Ninive. "You saw Hugo took Idomenea?" I told her at some point. "Well . . . yeah . . . He's not going to leave her here, with you and those soldiers," she replied. "Why?" "You haven't noticed their faces? They frighten me a bit, I try not to be alone. Now, whenever you head out, I'll stay in the room and lock it." "Really? They scare you that much?" "No, it's not just the fear. It's that I don't feel safe. Everything changed a lot and too suddenly. Before, even though it was worse, I knew what to expect each day, I even knew what Anibal would do to me and it didn't frighten me, only angered me a bit. Now what am I? What must I do? And what are you?" I laughed and she continued, looking serious: "No, I mean it. Who are you? When will you leave? At times I think that at any moment you'll go and leave me here alone. And then, what will I do? Idomenea left with Hugo . . . The old servant will die at any moment . . . You're leaving . . . These guys could kill you at any moment and then . . ." I embraced her and told her not to worry, that everything would be fine, but, while I said those things, I was disturbed by the idea that she could be right. Meanwhile, she cried a little and repeated, "Everything is so unstable."

I left her lying down on the bed and went out to look for Justino in his room. He wasn't there. I went out to the garden and saw him smelling some flowers. "Justino, how's it going?" I said. "Good, good, over here, with nature." "I see. Where are the others?" "Please, don't speak to me of the others." "Why?" "I don't know, they found a book lying around and are messing around with that . . ." "What book?" "Look, here they come . . ." And there the four of them were, coming out of the forest, jumping and nudging each other, laughing hysterically. When they arrived, I told them we had a job to do, that it was the job I had told them about in the morning; there were three storehouses, and that after it was done we could rest free and easy. We went up to a room, which was close to the kitchen and grabbed fuel, explosives, matches, shovels, and axes; then we grabbed masks, goggles, boots, and gloves and left to the first slave quarters. Suddenly, a very dense and dark cloud covered the sky. "How scary!" one of the soldiers said in a mocking tone, and the other three laughed, and went on like that making jokes the rest of the way. But when we arrived at the storehouse and they saw what was inside, they were mute. "Is this where you . . . ?" one asked me. "Yes, here I . . ." I said. "And they forced you to . . . ?" another asked me. "Yes they forced me to . . ." I said. "And for hours you . . . ?" another asked me. "Yes, for hours I . . ." I said. And the fourth asked me: "And now we're going to . . . ?" "Yes, we're going to . . ." I said. Then the four vomited in unison. "I'm leaving," said Justino. "You're not leaving," I said, "we're going to do away with this place so nobody, ever, will have to . . ." So then we began to work: we made room, doused fuel on everything, put down explosives, and left; once outside, some hundred yards away, we lit the fuse. We heard the explosion while arriving at the second storehouse and saw fire rising up through the air, and we celebrated, but stopped celebrating when we entered the new storehouse, which was bigger and even more putrid and repugnant than the last. "And the next one is bigger?" asked one. "Yes, but it's the last one," I said. We did the same things as before, but this time it was more work and we couldn't avoid getting dirty, vomiting, fainting; although they were suffering, I was happy: it was the same work I had once been forced to do, but from a very different perspective. As we were arriving at the third storehouse, we saw the second storehouse explode. Since it had gotten very dark, the explosion, bigger than the last one, turned out to be impressive and even beautiful, and so we celebrated along the way. And, once again, we stopped celebrating when we entered the third storehouse. "No, no, I'm leaving!" shouted Justino, and the other four grabbed him and prevented him from doing so. "Come on, it's the last one!" I told him. And we worked in a way that might make one think of humiliation but in reality it was the complete opposite; that, at least, was what I tried to make them understand: that this work was work in the name of freedom; "the proof of this," I told them, "is that it won't be possible to do after we're done." Every now and then, one of us would faint; then someone would grab whoever it was and take them out for air. We were there for a long time until everything was ready, and we watched this last explosion from a stream we had gone into to clean up a bit, although thanks to the gloves, boots, etc., we hadn't really gotten dirty at all. The spectacle of the explosion made us splash around with joy. We were exhausted but happy; at least I was very happy. The flames of the three storehouses burning illuminated the sky, and while Justino and I looked on, fascinated, behind us the other four were laughing, pushing each other, and it seemed to me in that moment, fondling and pinching each other underwater.

When we returned to the castle, Ninive and the old servant were at the door, waiting. Ninive was furious and frightened, but calmed down immediately when I embraced her. After eating something in the room and talking a bit, we fell asleep.

CHAPTER 15

THE NEXT DAY, I woke up coughing. Ninive was sleeping face down, uncovered, and with her nightgown lifted up; I pulled it back down and covered her with the sheet. I was surprised to see that breakfast wasn't on the nightstand. There was a strange, strong smell, a little like something burning, which I assumed was coming from the storehouses. There wasn't much light; I went to the window, opened it, and then shut it, horrified. Through the glass, I saw that the garden was completely gray, covered with a layer of ash that rippled like liquid; the ash also swept through the air darkening everything. "Ninive," I said, still looking out the window, "wake up." "What's going on?" she said, coughing. "Look," I said, pointing outside. She drew near, looked, and, without saying anything, embraced me and put her head on my shoulder. We put on some robes and went to the kitchen. The door to the outside had been left open: everything was covered in ash, and for some reason there wasn't any running water. "Perhaps because of the explosion," I told Ninive. "Maybe the pipes are clogged," she said. We saw the old servant sitting on a chair:

she appeared to be sleeping, but was dead. Then Ninive, with teary eyes, asked me what we would do. "Nothing," I told her, "wait for the ash to settle down and go away." "It won't go away," she replied, serious and despondent. "What's wrong with you? What do you mean it won't go away?" I asked her. "I knew this would go wrong, I told you so." "*What* did you tell me?" "I told you I was afraid, that I had dreamed awful things." I didn't respond. We returned to our room, I left Ninive there and went down. The front door of the castle was ajar. I peeked out and saw Justino. "I told you," he said. "Told me what?" I asked indignantly. "No, I didn't tell you anything, but there was a reason I didn't want to do what we did last night." "You didn't want to because it was disgusting." "Well, yes, it was disgusting and I wanted to leave because of that; in fact, I'm marked for life by the scene you put me in; but actually, although I didn't realize it at the time, I didn't want to do it because I knew something like this would happen. And wasn't I right? Look at what we have now. Ash, black ash everywhere covering everything. Breathing and swallowing are difficult, your mouth dries up and your eyes run with tears. There's no water or light. This is death. Before, the decay was contained in three places; all you had to do was straighten it out every now and then; now it's spread across the gardens, streams, forests . . ." And when he said forests I thought of the wild girl. I imagined her having trouble breathing, without being able to find food or water, curled up in a treetop full of ash, and felt shame and guilt. "What are we going to do now?" Justino asked me. "We're going to wait for the ash to go away," I said. "Sorry, but the ash isn't going away." "Not going away?" I shouted at him.

He looked at me: "Come, look," he said, and made a gesture to follow him. We skirted the castle to one of the corners, and from there I saw the three huge and towering columns of fire and black smoke that, like giant chimneys, scattered the decay that was burning in the storehouses. Without looking at me, Justino then said: "It could last for days. Who would even think of burning something like that?" "I would. Look, if the ash doesn't go away we'll leave as soon as Hugo's messenger arrives and we'll relocate to the other castle," I said, a little irritated. "That sounds better, but it'll have to be soon." "It'll be soon, don't worry, and relax a little." "I'm relaxed, but, with all due respect, I'm older than you and have more experience." "Older? At most you're three years older." "Fine, but they're three years." "Yes, what I mean to say is that it doesn't seem like enough." "Perhaps . . . ," he said. "And where are the other four?" I asked. "I don't know, I don't have the slightest idea nor do I care," he said. "Justino, listen closely: those four are under your charge." "I don't want them under my charge." "Well, it doesn't matter what you want, they're under your charge. I'll see you later." I left him and went back to my room.

Ninive wasn't there. For some reason, I assumed she'd be in the kitchen and went there. "What are you doing?" I said when I saw her. "Can't you see?" she replied without looking at me. She had laid the old servant down, taken off her clothes, and was cleaning her with a rag. "What are you doing?" I asked again. "*What are you doing? What are you doing?* Enough, is that all you can say?" she said, without looking at me and in a very disagreeable tone. I approached. "Do you want us to bury her?" I asked, and put my hand on her waist, which she immediately and roughly brushed off. "What do you think? She was a good woman; for me, in certain moments, like a mother, or at least an aunt. She died during a difficult time and I want to give her the burial she deserves. Come on, help me, please," and she picked up a white dress from the floor and, with difficulty, we started to put it on her. Since it was difficult, I grabbed the body by the armpits and lifted it up while Ninive lifted the dress, which almost didn't fit, over her; but when she had the dress up to the waist, my arms tightened and the body slipped and fell to the floor with a horrible sound. Ninive looked at me with a face full of hatred, which up to that moment I didn't think possible, while I asked for forgiveness and tried lifting the servant. "You're an idiot! You mess everything up!" she screamed. I didn't say anything: I placed the body back on the table and arranged it with falsely loving gestures, more directed toward Ninive than the old servant. Ninive then took lipstick and mascara out of a pouch. "What are you doing?" I asked. "Enough with your 'What are you doings'!" she screamed. "Where did you get these things, the dress, the makeup?" I asked. "They were in the wardrobe in Anibal's room. I assume they belonged to his wife." "Oh." With a care so exaggerated that it seemed demented, Ninive horribly and excessively applied makeup to the old servant. Then she took a few steps back, looked at the results and said: "Please, I want you to bury her, not those disgusting soldiers." "Me, alone? Have you looked outside?" "It's all I ask of you, can't you do it for me?" she said nervously and left.

Seated there, I thought about what Hugo might be doing and about what I was doing, about my situation and about his, that is, I compared myself to him, and the result of the comparison left me despondent and made me think that I was making the wrong decisions and letting go of the little power that at a certain moment I had achieved, and the little love that I had begun to receive. I went out by the castle door. Justino was still there. "What are you doing?" I asked him. "Sorry," he said. "What?" "Sorry I treated you badly." "You didn't treat me badly," I replied, a little annoyed. "No, well, whatever: I'm at your service." I asked him to help me with the burial, but that seemed to annoy him: "Again with those things? Why don't you leave everything as is?" I held my ground: "Weren't you in my service?" "Yes, yes, let's just do it." We then went to look for the body. When Justino saw it, he shook his head in a disapproving manner. "What?" I asked him. "I feel sorry for the lady . . . Who made her up like this?" I didn't respond. We lifted her, placed her in a bag, and left through the kitchen door. Upon leaving, I saw the three huge and towering columns of fire and black smoke that, like giant chimneys, scattered the decay that was burning in the storehouses. "They're bigger," said Justino. "You think?" "Yes, they're bigger and will keep growing." I looked at them: they had taken on the shape of black tubes; from the ends, the ash was surging upward forming swirls and other figures. We laid the body on the floor. "Now what?" Justino asked. "We have to bury her," I replied. "We don't have shovels," he said. "So why don't you go look for one?" I said. "One or two?" he said, smiling. "Bring whatever you find." He left and came back with two shovels. We decided to bury her right there, at the edge of the castle. By the time we set to work, we were already covered in ash, coughing, and tearing up. We had only dug two shallow holes, which didn't connect. Ash was flying everywhere and we were unable to see. "And the body?" I asked Justino. We moved dirt and ash around for a while; since the body didn't show, Justino said: "She's already buried then." I agreed, saying we really couldn't do more; we flattened the ground a little with the shovels and returned to the kitchen, but I felt bad, and so I went to search for the corpse as soon as he left. I searched for a long time and didn't find it, and that made me feel worse.

I grabbed something to eat in the kitchen and went up to my room. Ninive had locked the door. I had to knock for a while before she opened. "What happened? Sleeping?" "No." "So why did you take so long to open the door?" She didn't respond. I put the food on the bed and made a gesture to Ninive to help herself. "That's disgusting," she said. "I don't see how," I said. "I don't know, look at it, it's disgusting, disgusting." I looked at the food: "I see it perfectly fine." "No, no, look closely, it's disgusting." The food was fine, so I told her that if she didn't want to eat, she shouldn't bother. When she saw me eat the first mouthful, she ran out of the room; soon after, I heard her vomiting in the bathroom. She came back. "What's wrong with you?" I asked. "I told you I found it disgusting, and you ate it anyway." "I'm hungry." "So why don't you go eat in the kitchen?" "Fine." I grabbed the food and went down. Justino was there, eating. "I have an idea," he told me: "let's go find the car, get in, and leave." "Where?" I asked. "To Hugo," he said. "The messenger still hasn't arrived," I said. "The messenger won't arrive, not with this ash." "He will," I said. "No, won't happen." And when I told him, "we'll see," there was a knock at the door. "Who is it?" I asked, and in came a man blackened, covered in ash, coughing, crying, hunched over; "conquered castle, family imprisoned," he said, panting, and fell over as if he were dead. I ran to him and shook him; then I checked his pulse. "Yes, he's dead," I said. "Well," Justino said, "now we can leave." "We have to bury him," I said. "Do it yourself, if you want," he said. With some guilt, I left the dead man there and went up to my room. "We're leaving!" I shouted at Ninive through the door. She opened immediately. "Seriously?" she asked. "Yes." Within fifteen minutes we were all at the castle's front door. Ninive was the only one who had any luggage. "What's in there?" I asked. She didn't say. "I'll go find the car," I said. "We won't all fit," said Ninive, and Justino and the other four looked at each other and then at me. "We will," I said, and went to find the car. When I reached the side of the castle, I saw the three huge and towering columns of fire and black smoke that, like giant chimneys, scattered the decay that was burning in the storehouses. It seemed as though they were growing and becoming more solid, they already looked like real chimneys. I went into the garage, got in the car, closed the convertible top, and took off. Attempting to back out, I miscalculated and scratched the whole side. I reached the castle door, and Ninive immediately got in the passenger's seat. The other four jumped in the back. Justino stood there, staring. "Squeeze in where you can," I told him. He looked at the four, then us, and asked: "Can I go in the front?" Although there was extra room because the car was wide, Ninive told him no, he should go in the back. Grumbling, he climbed in the back while the other four laughed. I didn't really know which way to go, but it seemed best not to say anything.

In any case, escaping the ash would be good enough; then we could figure it out. And so I took off in the direction that Hugo had taken with his troops.

The ash flew everywhere and blocked my view. Every so often I had to get out to clean the windshield. Five minutes after leaving, the ash had gotten worse: probably due to the humidity and the swirling winds, it had begun to congeal and form massy objects, like worms made of ash that leaped violently upon us and the car. And I truly didn't know where to go. But I kept driving anyway, until there was a loud bang and the car stopped. I got out and saw that the worms had gotten in between the wheels, inside the motor, in the exhaust pipe . . . When I announced that we should abandon the car, Ninive started insulting me, which encouraged Justino to insult me as well. The other four, however, just laughed. "What are you laughing at?" Justino asked them, suddenly more irritated with them than with me, but they didn't respond because they were too busy giving each other playful pinches and pulling down each other's pants. This irritated Justino so much that he leapt at them and started throwing punches. I leapt at Justino, but I wasn't quick enough, and two out of the four were left with bloody faces. Afterward, I had to convince Ninive to leave her luggage behind: "We can only take weapons and some food," I told her. And then, all of a sudden, we heard an incredibly loud noise coming from the still-visible castle: a mountain of ash covered half the structure and was collapsing one of the towers. Off to the side, three huge and towering columns of fire and black smoke scattered, like giant chimneys, the decay that was burning in the storehouses, and the storehouses themselves, which continued to slowly burn.

CHAPTER 16

I NEVER FELT so close to death as I did during those two days of walking through the ash and the ash worms, which, growing more and more intelligent, jumped in our faces and got under our clothes. With hardly any food and no water at all, our only pastime was to continually complain; Ninive, in fact, went practically the whole way crying and regretting having worn a skirt. At one point, Justino died: he choked on a worm that got in his mouth just as another sealed his nose, and since we didn't have shovels, we had to leave his body behind, which in any case was immediately buried by the ash. From then on, the fear of death accompanied us the entire journey; even the attitude of the four soldiers underwent a change; they laughed, but the laughs were shorter, as if they were embarrassed to hear them. And it was shortly after this that, almost defeated by the situation, I kneeled on the ground, rested my head against the ash and sang, aloud, the only prayer I had learned as a child: "Please, God, help me to overcome incongruities." When they saw and heard me do this, Ninive and the four soldiers wanted to join in, and asked me to teach them this prayer. And so, holding each other's hands, we sang: "Please, in this incongruity / I have this made-up prayer for you / good God / we suffer decadence / etc." As soon as we finished, Ninive fainted; luckily, the others immediately offered to carry her. They carried her in twos, taking turns, for almost three hours. When Ninive awoke, she cursed them out, accused them of touching her, and swore not to talk to me ever again for allowing such a thing. She talked to me, though, two hours later, when, coming out of a very long, narrow, curved, and well-constructed tunnel that went through a mountain chain, we appeared in a green prairie, with fruit trees and little animals. The mountains, apparently, functioned as a barrier against the ash. We jumped for joy, embraced each other, picked fruit, ate it, and took a dip in a lake. The six of us, that is, the four soldiers, Ninive, and I.

We were in the lake, Ninive and I; the four soldiers had already left a while ago to explore the area. So I hugged her, because she was still a little upset with me, and that softened her up a bit: she apologized for having treated me poorly, and gave me a hug and a kiss. But at the same time, she appeared to be quite distressed, and it was clear that she was making an enormous effort to remain calm and, so to speak, normal, that is, how she used to be. We were in the lake, in a cavity between very high rock walls, and I kissed her back, once, twice, three times, until we let ourselves be carried away by our desire. Soon after, we lay down naked and exhausted on a smooth rock and, looking up, toward the top edge of the rock walls, we saw something strange, which Ninive was the first to identify: it was the heads of the four soldiers looking down at us. Ninive then started to cry and scream, in the middle of some sort of a nervous breakdown, and I shouted at the four to come down and quickly gave Ninive her clothing and put my own back on. When they appeared in front of us, Ninive was still naked, and so I shouted at them to turn around, and covered her; then I told them off, I even slapped one, who looked like he was about to burst out laughing, but Ninive already had a blank stare, and I noticed that I didn't care, that I was telling them off for her: they saw us, they didn't see us, what difference did it make? Besides, they explained that their intention wasn't to spy on us, that they had climbed up a slope until reaching that overlook and that, looking down, they'd been surprised to see us there and had kept staring at us without understanding what we were doing. I left them and went back over to Ninive. "Ninive, what's going on?" I said, and for some reason, seeing her like that, I almost called her Nini. She didn't say anything. Then I deliberately tried to be more affectionate and call her "Nini," but couldn't, because something caught in my throat. "Ninive, what's up?" I said again, but she looked off to the side. She wasn't mad or anything like that: she was gone, beyond this situation. From that moment on, Ninive became a ghost. Or no, not even a ghost: an old rag, someone without agency and whom one had to care for, because on her own she was incapable of taking any initiative, including something as fundamental as feeding oneself. Not that you had to put food in her mouth, no; what you had to do was bring the food close to her and say: "Please eat." She would then, slowly and despondently, eat a little. Internally, I wanted to blame the four soldiers for spying on us, but was it just? They had been a little stupid, sure, but what they had done in no way presupposed what ended up happening. At the same time, they'd acted out of pure restlessness and curiosity, without malice. Could I blame them for an unexpected and unimaginable effect of what they had done? I didn't think so, and somehow that decision made me feel affection toward them.

We spent several days like this, walking through meadows and highlands, always surrounded by water and fruit trees. The ash had been definitively left behind, and our lungs were, little by little, becoming clean. We hunted animals with our shotguns; and the meat was accompanied by a mix of vegetables that were new to us. In any case, the four soldiers mostly just talked among themselves, and on top of that, always in a whisper. Ninive walked along, but she was absent and disinterested. It was then that I had time to think, and I came to enjoy the act of thinking while walking through pleasant surroundings, and perhaps because of that I wasn't overly enthused when we heard distant sounds and shouts and saw a post with a shield nailed to it alerting us that we were approaching a castle. Nor was I enthused when we noticed that the emblem on the shield was very similar to the one at Anibal's castle, and carried his family name. Nor when, to remove all doubt about the outcome of Hugo's battle, a naked woman appeared, followed by a man whom I recognized as one of our soldiers; the woman was laughing heartily, and the man chased after her with obvious sexual desire; but he was fat and lame and she was beautiful and athletic, and as a result he would never catch up with her unless she let him. After this, we caught the smell of decay, and reached a bridge that crossed a stream: it was the entrance bridge to the castle's territory, but the territory was so big that we couldn't yet see the castle. When we looked down from the bridge, we saw that the stream was dammed by an enormous pile of decomposing bodies. We all vomited, except Ninive, who appeared to neither see nor smell anything. And then, as we crossed the bridge, we saw two hanging corpses, a woman and a man. The woman's face didn't reveal anything, but when I saw the man's I realized that the two who'd been hanged were Anibal's son and his wife. "Ninive, this is horrible," I said, but she didn't respond. The four soldiers were solemn, as if they'd been told not to laugh, or better yet, as if they'd seen something they didn't imagine possible. We kept walking, coming across more and more soldiers. And just when we were starting to see the tip of a castle tower, one of the soldiers recognized me and shouted, "It's the king," and that drew the attention of several other soldiers; those soldiers, about eight of them, lifted me onto a chair and took me, all the while singing, to Hugo; along the way I noticed that the son's castle was very different from the father's: there were many women, several of them sensually dressed; there was a huge swimming pool; and also spaces for recreation, sports, etc., and many children playing; that's to say, there were lots of people, hundreds of them going from one place to another, doing various things, like . . .

The soldiers set me down in the middle of a crowd that had joined them along the way; the crowd shouted, "Long live the king," and some added, "Die oppressor pigs!" And it wasn't just our old soldiers who were shouting: many were from the son's castle, that is, the newly freed. That made me happy. Hugo emerged skipping from the crowd and embraced me. The people shouted, "Long live the king and Captain Hugo." While hugging, we told each other things: I told him, "Congratulations," and he told me, "You too, King"; and I told him, "This is incredible," and he said, "We're achieving it." Then we released each other, the crowd dispersed still clapping, and, apart from Hugo, only my four accompanying soldiers remained. Ninive was missing. "Where's Ninive?" I asked the four. They looked at one another, shrugged their shoulders, and shook their heads, while showing me the palms of their hands. "Seriously, you don't know?" I asked them again. They remained silent. "Well, look for her, please," I said, and they took off running. "I don't say please anymore," said Hugo when we were alone. "I'm worried, there are lot of people and Ninive was acting very strange," I said. "What's happening will change history," he said. "And if I never find her?" I said, and we remained quiet awhile. During this time I calmed down and thought that Ninive must be around here somewhere and would reappear soon. Hugo asked me why I had left Anibal's castle. I quickly explained what had happened, omitting the major disasters; that is, I barely mentioned the ash and told him, instead, that for me Anibal's castle was tainted by the idea of slavery. "Of course," he said. Then I made him understand that I had set it on fire, and when he was about to ask something, I said: "So, how did the battle go?" "Oh, incredible. Only three of ours died, and two of those three deaths occurred after the battle, I still don't understand how. The other side lost sixty or seventy." "Really? So many?" I asked, shocked. "Yes, it was due to the roots, which had an incredible effect: we all became strong and crazy," he told me. "But you killed seventy people?" I asked, impressed. "Yes, but it wasn't our fault. Anibal's son, whose name turned out to be . . . I don't remember his name. Anibal's son promised freedom to the slaves who would fight against us. Can you believe it? Fight against those who want to free you in exchange for the promise of liberation . . . ! The ones who died had taken that offer; the rest immediately joined us, and there were hundreds of them. They'd been waiting for us, I don't know how they found out. I think they'd been informed by those teenagers who'd stayed with us and asked for permission to go to the city. Then we won the battle right away. Almost without fighting. But we had already eaten the roots, and when the slaves who had joined us handed over the ones who had taken the offer from . . ." "They were shot?" I asked, already upset. "No, no . . . Actually, I don't know what happened. At that moment, I lost control and later they'd been killed." "I can't believe it . . . You seriously killed them all?" "No, Anibal's son and wife were hanged by their ex-slaves." "And the children?" "I don't know." "What do you mean you don't know? You killed them too?" "No, well, I think they're in the forest," he said, and pointed to the forest. Then I looked and saw a group of liberated children throwing rocks toward the forest. "What are they doing?" "They won't let them return," Hugo said. "Who? Anibal's son's children?" "Mmhmm." "So then they're alive . . ." "Yes, yes, we don't kill children . . ." There was a silence, and then I said: "And couldn't you have buried them?" "Who?" "The ones you killed; I saw them back there, piled up under the bridge." He stared at me: "Didn't you see the state they're in and the smell they give off?" I stared back: "Obviously, they're like that *now*. What I'm saying is that you could have buried them before they decomposed." He then lowered his gaze and said: "Yes, I know. I proposed throwing them into the stream. I thought the water would carry them away. But it seems that one got stuck to a branch and they started piling up, right there under the bridge . . ." "Well, I'm going to order they be buried." He stared at me again, but this time with a pleading expression: "No, please! You'll put my authority on the line. I already told them we wouldn't bury them and that they deserved it for being traitors!" My answer was, "I don't care, we have to bury them." Then I left to gather people: I stood on a platform and shouted, "I need volunteers for a job." Immediately, dozens of people approached me, almost all of them from the castle. I took advantage of this and told them I was proud of what we had accomplished, that we were assisting the first stage of the definitive liberation of all the slaves on the planet, and that nothing could hold us back from continuing with this, and even going further.

Among the volunteers were the four soldiers who had arrived with me. I asked them if they'd found Ninive, even though judging by their faces I could tell they hadn't. I gathered the group together and explained what had to be done. At the beginning they refused, and the only way of convincing them was to reassure them that I, too, would work. Still, some of them declined, begging me not to punish them for it. I told them they were free, they could do whatever they wanted, including not doing what was good for them. When I said that, a few more left. Since there was no cemetery, I founded one, behind the castle; I named it "The End" and ordered an enormous sign to be carved in wood. When we reached the bridge, I quickly looked among the bodies; for some reason, I was afraid I'd find Ninive there. She was so strange and vulnerable that it seemed possible she had killed herself. This matter disturbed me deeply, but since I truly believed she might be circling around nearby, I wasn't completely anguished. Here's what I thought: if she needs some time, she should take it; if she doesn't want to be with me anymore, I'll find another, for there were plenty and more beautiful ones to choose from here.

We went down to the stream from the bank. When we came to the water, many vomited. The smell was unbearable, and the bodies were far more decomposed than I'd thought. "Let's go, boys, we're doing the right thing," I shouted, and approached the first body with a bag. This encouraged the others, and in an hour all the bodies were bagged. The smell, nevertheless, persisted, and after carrying the decaying corpses we were steeped in it. And just when I thought we would have to drag the body bags up to the cemetery, which was some five hundred yards away, Hugo showed up driving a van. "Long live Captain Hugo!" they all shouted, and he got out and helped us load the bodies into the van.

Once in the cemetery, we had a discussion: Hugo wanted to make a communal ditch; I wanted to verify the names of everyone and bury them in their own plots with a gravestone. What I did accept was that there would be only one ritual for all the dead, but Hugo had another opinion on this matter, too: there shouldn't be a ritual. I was on the verge of saying, "I'm the king, I decide"; fortunately I did something else: I gathered as many people as I could and expounded the two positions in an emotional speech on the rights of those slaves who died deceived: "They have the right to be buried with dignity, and only that will calm their ghosts," I said, and some women cried. Then, Hugo, spoke of the "disgust" that the "traitors" made him feel, and his speech would have worked if it hadn't been for a joke made by one of the four soldiers who had arrived with me: when Hugo said, "They disgust me," the soldier shouted from the crowd: "That's because they're rotten." Then everyone laughed and started chanting: "Bury them!" So it was decided, and so it was done. We dug very deep graves; delicately placed the bodies in, and filled the holes with heavy rocks and soil. The physical labor distracted us all from the decaying smell. The shared ritual was moving, above all because of the emotional things that were said: the wife of one man spoke, then the friend of another one, the son of yet another . . . Each of the deceased had someone who missed them.

CHAPTER 17

THE NEXT DAY, I woke up in my new room, which was the room of the previous owners but completely redecorated, and the first thing I saw was breakfast on the nightstand. I reached for the kettle and noticed it was warm. I stood up and went to the window. It was a pleasant day, neither hot nor cold, and below, in the garden, hundreds of people were coming and going: women with children, couples in love, groups of men. A little farther on, in the swimming pool, there were lots of people playing and enjoying themselves. And even farther, in the recreational spaces, some people ran and jumped around; I looked toward the forest: a group of children threw rocks at two boys and a girl hiding in the trees. They were Anibal's son's children. I thought this wasn't right, and that I should fix it, but I didn't see how. Those children, raised as slave owners, with all of their luxuries and whims, wouldn't be comfortable among us. At the same time, they were very young, and there was still the possibility that they would be quick to adapt. The other option was to not do anything: in that case, they would probably die; if not, they would turn feral. I thought about the wild girl and my mood darkened, and just at that moment there was a knock on the door. I thought about Ninive, about whether they had found her, dead or alive. I said, "Come in," and a soldier entered to inform me that Captain Hugo wanted to see me urgently in the dining room. Hugo was still a little resentful about the success of the ritual and his error of judgment, which was grave: looking upon the cheated as traitors.

I went down and they served me breakfast again, but this time it was very luxurious, clearly what the previous owners used to eat. "You ordered this for me?" I asked Hugo. "No, it's the custom here," he replied. "What? They all eat like this?" I asked. "No, I don't think so," he said. "Then it's not right," I said, upset, and angrily threw the breakfast at the floor. Immediately four young servants appeared. "First of all," I told them, "you're no longer servants. Secondly, I want to have the same breakfast as you." "Okay," said one with a very attractive and teasing smile, and promptly brought me tea and bread. "Perfect, thanks," I said, but at the same time I regretted not having at least some of the things from the previous breakfast. "I want to discuss two matters with you," Hugo said. "You don't eat breakfast?" I asked. "Yes, I already ate." "Oh." "Okay, two things. First, something that worries me. I want to make sure you're not going to want to bury the hanged." "What?" "Just that, that you won't want to bury them." "Um, okay, that's fine . . . I suppose . . ." "What do you mean *suppose*?" "I mean it occurs to me that at some point they're going to have to be buried." "No!" "Why?" "Because I told everyone we'd leave them there to rot." "And why did you say that?" I asked. "Because it seemed like a good image." "Yes, perhaps . . . But, what then? You're going to leave the skeletons there forever?" "No, no." "Well then, something must be done." "Like what?" "Perhaps a different kind of ritual that'll reinforce the image you proposed." "Perhaps . . . Fine, secondly, I wanted to tell you that Calambra . . ." "Calambra?" I asked. "Yes, the one I introduced you to at the castle, the short one I picked as second in command." "Ah, yes." "Well, Calambra is going to head out tomorrow toward another castle with a troop of one hundred." "Wow! That's great!" "Yes, yes, it was kind of his idea." "So, which castle?" "A bigger one, it's nearby." "Well, perfect. And they're not training?" "Yes, they're behind the castle, we'll go see them later. Many of them want to meet you." "Perfect." "And a third thing." "You said two." "Yes, I got confused . . . Well, the third is that there's a problem with one of the four men you arrived with." "Oh, yes?" "Yes." "And what's the problem?" "I didn't really understand, but apparently one of them tried to rape, or raped, or hurt trying to rape, or hurt trying to do something else, another man." "When, where?" "Last night, at a bonfire they made to celebrate your arrival." "So now what?" "Well, the problem is that apparently in this castle the slaves were permanently punished for whatever reason, and so now there are many people demanding his punishment." "Really?" "Yes, but not only that: they want us to kill him, to shoot him, and some even want for all four to be shot because they're not sure which of the four it was." "Really? We . . . we won't do it, and order somebody to tell them that whoever touches any one of the four men I came with will be exiled from the castle. And also to tell them that no one has the right to kill anyone. No, not that: they should be told that no one can kill anyone, like a law, and that they're no longer slaves, and that each individual is responsible for their actions." Hugo looked at me like he didn't understand: "I can't have somebody tell them that . . ." "Why?" "You don't understand, if we don't kill him ourselves, they'll kill him, and there's a lot of them, and we can't just exile them all." I remained silent, and then said: "Fine, I'll come up with something else . . . For the time being, gather the four and tell them to hide in my room." "In your room?" "Mmm. No, better not, in another room, then. But they should hide."

Hugo sent someone to do these things, and then we went out to see the soldiers who were preparing for battle. It was an impressing spectacle. "Now this is an army," I told Hugo. "Captain Hugo! King!" shouted Calambra, and ran over to us. He was shorter than I remembered, only coming up to our waists, but he had a strong, brawny voice, and spoke at full volume, which turned out to be perfect for coordinating the hundred soldiers. "This all looks good," I told Calambra. "Thanks, we've been working very hard." And having said this he returned to them. He shouted, "forward," "down," "close," "black turn," "silence," "blip," and with each word all one hundred did something very precise at the same time. It resembled a choreography like the ones . . . In the back were the soldiers with the strange weapons, but there were more than last time. "What about them?" I asked Hugo. "Oh, you wouldn't believe it. They do incredible things with those weapons." Satisfied, we left. Calambra shouted, "Bye," and the soldiers jumped, all at once.

I told Hugo that at night we would send the soldiers off with a party, and that at this party we would burn the hanged. He agreed.

CHAPTER 18

AT THE CLIMAX of the party that night, when we burned the bodies, which already smelled terrible, the ash and the smell forced us to move the tables and chairs, and transfer the dance floor and the stage for the musicians. "That wasn't right," said Hugo. "Perhaps," I replied as I watched the wind carry the ash toward the forest, so that there was the possibility that the dead parents' ashes would settle on the skin of their living children. This image disturbed me, but not only the image: I was disturbed by the ash and, above all, by the realization that when planning this ritual I hadn't taken the ash into account; this neglect worried me: if I could forget this, I could also forget many other important things. In any case, this mistake hadn't had serious consequences and the party was a success: hundreds of people danced, drank, laughed . . . A woman approached me in that moment. She was the ex-servant who had smiled flirtatiously at me during breakfast. I greeted her and she offered me a drink that lifted my spirits and excited me, for which reason I continued drinking all night, feeling more and more animated and exuberant. In this state, I told

Hugo a little more about what had happened at the castle
after burning the storehouses, although I gave few details
and kept it very ambiguous and vague, so much so that many
of the things I said sounded like metaphors: "to burn what
caused pain," "the ash of decay hid the sun," etc. And when
Hugo wanted to know more, perhaps also animated by drink,
instead of answering him, I began to feel sad over Ninive.
"Well, maybe she wasn't the one for you," he said. "What?
She was perfect, we got along really well, we loved each other
. . ." I said. "Well, the truth is that . . ." "What?" "No, nothing." "Hugo, tell me." "No, it's not important. What I'm
saying is that maybe she wasn't such a good woman, I don't
know." I insisted and Hugo ended up confessing that Ninive
had slept in his bed many times. "Slept? Nothing more?"
"No, well, you know . . ." "You mean that . . ." "Yes, sorry."
This dialogue, which ended there, disturbed me and made
me drink in a now-uncontrolled way. And so, at some point,
I joined a group that was chatting about something. When
they noticed me, the group immediately went silent. "Go on,
relax, keep chatting," I said, but they didn't talk and looked at
me with pity, because I was already very drunk. And I don't
know how, but I think someone made an innocent joke that
bothered me, and I, trying to demonstrate in a friendly way
that there were limits, head-butted his nose, which clouded
my vision, and I fell to the ground. There was silence, and
when I stood up I saw that the other man had passed out,
with a smashed-in nose and a bloody face. Hugo ran up to
me and grabbed me by the shoulders, but I got loose, shouted
"No one grabs me, I'm loose!" and took off walking until I
got lost in the forest.

CHAPTER 19

I WOKE UP somewhere, surrounded by trees. It was daytime. Three children, a little dirty and very small, were sleeping around me. It was then I remembered vaguely and in bits and pieces that they and I had been running around and playing in the forest all night long, and that they were Anibal's children. I stood up carefully so as not to disturb them. I remembered the previous night; I touched my forehead and felt a bump. I thought about the possibility of taking them back to the castle, but immediately abandoned it. I walked for ten minutes and left the forest. I was a few yards from the swimming pool. Although still dizzy, I walked up to its edge; everyone inside silently stared at me. And then, amid the buzzing of "the king . . . the king . . . the king . . . ," I slipped and fell into the pool, and even though I began to drown and flail around, they all just looked at me without doing anything. I shouted, "Help! Help!" and just as I was going under, a hand grabbed me by my clothes, lifted me in the air, and laid me on the ground, on my back. My eyes were closed and, for some reason, I couldn't talk or move; suddenly I felt a mouth on my mouth, air that filled my lungs, and pressure on my chest, and then I spit water. When I opened my eyes, a woman was looking at me up-close. Around her, there was a crowd of people whispering. "Are you okay?" she asked. "Yes," I said, and when she smiled I realized it was the ex-servant who had brought me breakfast and had given me the drink the previous night. Between a few of them, they helped to lift me; once standing, they all shouted: "Long live the king!" It was a restrained shout: they still loved me, but now they feared me a little.

When I arrived at the castle, supported by the woman, whose name was Sumenela, I already felt well. Sumenela said farewell, and as I watched her go I felt that I liked her and that she was superior to Ninive in every way, and that, actually, any woman was better than Ninive and it was lucky that Hugo's revelation had brought the spell she had on me to an abrupt stop. I thought about seducing Sumenela, but realized in that moment that without Ninive's spell I felt numb and didn't need any woman. I went to see the soldiers behind the castle. I called Calambra and asked him when they would depart. "This evening, when the sun sets," he replied. "Perfect," I said, "I want you to take the four soldiers who arrived with me. They are brave men who . . ." "No . . . Please . . . ," he interrupted. "What's wrong?" "No, nothing, it's fine, I'll take them, but I have to ask you for something." "Tell me." "We have different roots that we've gathered from the surrounding areas, but they're very different from the ones at the other castle, and that worries me a little." "Want me to have a look?" "Yes, please." Then he took me aside and showed them to me. "How lovely," I said. Some were red, furry, and slimy, soft and fleshy on the outside, but with a very thin core, like a bone you could feel when you squeezed them; they seemed to be from another planet, and possibly they were. They were similar to but not exactly the same as the previous ones. There were also blue ones, with eye-like dots on top and bird-like legs at the base. Others, which were thinner, looked like a bunch of fluorescent threads. There were some that were a black ball, a little soft, and some that looked like the yellowish worms that appear on corpses. A few, finally, seemed to be moving. "Those aren't roots," I told him. He grabbed them, looked at them closely, and told me I was right, they weren't roots. "But what are they?" he asked. "I have no idea, but toss them, just in case." When he threw them on the ground, they quickly disappeared into the soil. Then I told him that the red ones were the most similar, but that I wasn't sure, and suggested he fight without the roots. "No, no, that's impossible. Not just for me, but for the others: they think they won because of the roots, and that without the roots we don't stand a chance." "And what do you think?" I asked. He looked at me: "I think the same . . . And you?" "It's possible . . . Well, eat those. I'll take the others, I want a closer look at them." Calambra agreed and told me that later someone would sort them out better, wash them, and bring them to my room. "Well, I wish you all a lot of luck," I said. "Thanks, everything's going to be fine." "I don't doubt it." I said farewell, feeling happy because of the roots, and because I had resolved the matter with those four strange and problematic soldiers whom I had grown fond of, whatever their faults. I went to find Hugo and told him that I didn't care about what he'd told me. "Phew . . . What a relief! I was worried . . ." he said. I explained that he had no cause to be, that he had been right in telling me, and I asked him about Idomenea. "Ah, she's doing great. It seems she's pregnant." "Really? Is it yours?" I asked. "Yes, of course, what are you trying to say?" he said, somewhere between annoyed and worried. "No, of course, I didn't mean anything, it was only a question."

My question had been innocent, but the question's effect had been my revenge. This revenge seemed to suffice, and I decided to try and forget the matter. And then I didn't know what to do and went out for a stroll. I walked a long distance; along the way I greeted many people, and without realizing it arrived at the bridge and looked down at the stream: it was clean and the smell was fading. That put me in a good mood. I walked a little more and climbed a hill. I looked for the path by which we had arrived at the castle and thought about many things; above all I thought about Ninive. In the distance, one could see a barrier of mountains, a type of small range. They were the mountains we had crossed by tunnel. The ash had remained behind these little mountains. Above the mountain range the sky was gray, and I thought of rain, but then immediately thought of the ash, and looked closer—it seemed to me that the gray of the sky had black spots, stains, and appeared to be moving. Then it seemed I was imagining this, that it was only a cloudy sky, and then I thought, I don't know why, that if we did things right, the ash wouldn't advance. I went down the hill, took a few steps, arrived at the bridge above the stream, looked at the clean stream running by, and couldn't help but say aloud: "How boring!" And when I said this, I surprised myself.

CHAPTER 20

WHEN I ENTERED my room, I saw the bag of roots on my bed. I emptied it on the floor and looked at them closely. There were blue ones, with some eye-like dots on top and bird-like legs at the base. Others, which were thinner, looked like a bunch of fluorescent threads. There were some that were a black ball, a little soft; when I applied a little pressure to one of these, the ball's shell cracked and a strongly scented black liquid started leaking out; I stored the ones that looked like the yellowish worms that appear on corpses in the bag again, because I found them disgusting, and then I put the balls away as well, because the smell was making me nauseous. I looked out the window and saw Hugo talking with Idomenea below. "Hugo, Hugo, come here!" I shouted. "Why?" he asked. "Come, come quickly," I insisted, and then he kissed Idomenea, who still didn't look pregnant, and came inside the castle. He knocked on my door. "Come in, come in." When he entered, I pointed to the roots on my bed and said, "Look." "What about them? Are those the ones we gathered with Calambra?" he asked. "Yes . . . what do you mean

what about them? That's what we have to find out." "What?"
"We have to try these roots and see what effects they have."
Hugo looked at me, nervous and surely not understanding
my enthusiasm. Feeling myself looked at this way, I realized
that my enthusiasm didn't even make sense to me. In any case,
the idea of trying these roots excited me, and so I insisted
until Hugo agreed. "And they won't be bad for us?" he asked,
in a last attempt to halt what was coming. "Bad? Mmm . . .
I hadn't thought of that . . . No, they won't be bad for us."
"How do you know?" "No, I don't know. Well, if you don't
want to, no problem." Hugo stood there thinking, and after
one minute of looking up at the ceiling, he said, with a smile:
"Sure, let's try them."

I don't know which was the order of what. What I can
say is that when I ate the first root, which was blue, with some
eye-like dots on top and bird-like legs at the base, I entered,
or we entered, a black hole in the middle of the void, and that
this only lasted a few minutes, although it's difficult to be
certain, and that after this we ate the blue root again, although
I might have also added some fluorescent threads, and so we
re-entered the black hole, which was the void, but a void
where something seemed to be preparing its appearance; this,
at least, was the feeling. We didn't understand, but at the same
time the effect made us curious, and so we ate them again,
and that time, upon exiting the black hole, we looked frightened, because, although the sensation was that while we were
in the black hole our body wasn't doing anything, upon leaving the hole I saw that Hugo was barefoot and that I had
climbed on top of the nightstand. "What happened?" I asked.
"I don't know, but it seems like we moved." "So while it

appears that we're in a black hole, in the middle of nothing, our body is here moving . . ." "It seems like that, yes." We waited awhile, but nothing happened: the effect was brief. That brevity relaxed us, and so then, I don't know why, we tried them again, and this time, upon leaving the back hole, Hugo was at my side, naked, and I had taken off my shirt. "This isn't right," I said, and immediately I was back in the black hole, and when I left, Hugo wasn't there, and neither were the roots. I looked at the room and it seemed unreal, or no, not unreal, but a different room, which kept changing while I wasn't there. Then Hugo walked in and told me that upon exiting the black hole he found himself in the garden. "I don't like this at all," he added. "Me neither, because it seems to be ongoing," I said while I re-entered the black hole; upon exiting, not only was Hugo not there but the window was broken. I looked out, then down. Hugo was thrown on the ground, surrounded by glass. I ran down shouting, but on my way I entered the black hole again, and, upon leaving it, I found myself alone in the pool, surrounded by people staring at me. "Are you okay?" asked a woman, who turned out to be Sumenela. "Yes, yes, all good," I said, and got out of the pool. Then Sumenela wrapped me in a towel and offered to accompany me to my room. "What happened?" I asked. "You don't know?" "No." She looked at me with a mixture of pity, fear, and maternal instinct and told me that I had jumped into the pool shouting that a hand was leading me there by the neck. "Really?" I asked. "Yes, and not only that: once you were in the pool, and everyone else got scared and left, you started saying that we all had to tear our handle out." "Our handle? What handle?" "I don't know, that's what you were shouting. I assume you were referring to the handle that the hand leading you into the pool was grabbing." "Oh," I said, and then I re-entered the black hole, and upon exiting I was in bed, naked, with Sumenela, also naked, at my side, smiling at me. "What happened?" I asked. "What?" she replied. "I'm asking *what happened?*" "You seriously don't remember anything?" she asked, visibly offended. "More or less," I said although in reality I didn't remember anything. "Let's see, what do you remember?" she asked, and then I entered the black hole again. When I left, I was still in the room, but was now sitting on the floor, contemplating a cup. "I don't think so," said Sumenela, who was sitting on the bed, dressed, smoking an enormous pipe. "What?" I asked. "I mean a handle, I don't have one," she replied. "What handle?" "Stop asking like that," she said. Then I looked at the cup and looked at the handle and the handle seemed strange. I entered the black hole again; upon leaving, I was still sitting with the cup, but this time the cup was broken and the handle had come loose; I had a notebook and a pen in my hands; in the notebook, I had written—it was my handwriting, that much was clear—the following: "The handle connects the cup's interior with the cup's exterior; at the same time, the handle is part of the cup. But if we remove the handle, only the interiority remains and the cup is unmanageable." I found the text completely foreign and at the same time very familiar. I approached Sumenela, who was still on the bed, and handed her the notebook: "What do you think?" She read it and said that it was good, but that it wasn't too original, that she herself had thought something similar at some point. "Well, perhaps," I said, and entered the black hole again. When I left,

I was on the bridge above the stream. For some reason, nothing about this black hole situation surprised me much: neither the changes in location, nor what I did when I was inside there, nothing. I was two people, but also just one, and although I didn't remember anything my other I did, this didn't strike me as strange either, just like how I didn't seem strange to the he who existed thanks to me. Although it could also be viewed the other way . . . I looked at the stream that flowed, it could be said, joyfully. Then I looked at the horizon: in front of me, the small mountain range was still crowned with ash, although it looked more like a cloudy sky. In that moment, I asked myself whether the ash and the columns of fire had been put out or whether, instead, the ash was accumulating behind the mountains. From there I walked back to the castle. On my way I found Idomenea, who asked me how I was. I told her fine and asked her if she knew where Hugo was, and as soon as I did, I remembered having seen him on the ground surrounded by glass and felt a kind of chill. Seeing me like that, she said: "Don't worry, I won't tell Hugo anything . . ." I looked at her: "What? About what?" She looked at me: "About what we did." "What we did?!" I shouted, looking aside for some reason. "Don't be stupid . . ." she said, sensually caressing my right arm. And there I entered the black hole. When I left, Hugo and I were sitting at the bottom of a well. I asked what we were doing there, and he replied: "All my skin is dead." I assumed Hugo was in the black hole at that moment, and asked him if that was the case. "What?" he said. "It seems like you're in the black hole," I repeated. He laughed: "No, no, I'm not, but you just got out." "And you? What are we doing here?" I asked. "I don't know, but the effect on me is fading: I'm going in less often now, and very lightly, so lightly that the black is a transparent gray and I can see what I'm doing . . . I see double . . . But it's lasting longer for you. Perhaps because of those fluorescent threads you ate." With difficulty, we got out of the well: he did; then me, with his help. And what I saw when I got out made me stop breathing: at least twenty unearthed bodies scattered among the graves. "What is this?" I asked. Hugo was pale. "I suppose we did that," he said. "That's all you have to say? It's terrible!" I said, furious. "Yes . . . No, it's not a big deal," he said. "You don't think so?" "No: before they were under there, now they're here. They're always in some place and they're always dead. What difference does it make?" I looked at him, serious: "The idea is that we don't have to see them." "Well, yes. But even if you don't see them, they're there," he said impassively. "It's not the same," I said, and we started to bury the bodies, but we didn't know which went where. "Who cares," Hugo said. "No!" I shouted. "What's the difference?" he asked with genuine curiosity. I didn't know what to say, and so we put them back at random. We wanted to finish before it got dark; at the same time, we were afraid of entering the black void in the middle of this task and ending up making a mess. A few yards away, five men were watching. I called them and asked them to bury the remaining bodies, claiming we had to get back to investigating something very important. No sooner had I said that than I entered the black hole. When I left, I was in the forest; in the distance, the sun was rising. I felt something on my back and tried scratching it, but a solid structure hooked to my shirt kept getting in the way. I took it off: it was a cardboard handle.

"Ugh, I can't do this anymore," I said aloud, and Anibal's son's children appeared. Now they looked more like the wild girl, and I felt sorry for them, but at the same time I was glad because it meant that they had adapted to their circumstances. "How's it going?" I asked. They smiled and offered me a piece of raw meat. "Oh, thanks," I said, because I realized I was hungry. While I ate the piece of meat, I noticed that I was barefoot and that my feet were very dirty. Evidently, I had been in the forest for a long time. Then I entered the black hole once more. When I left, even though I was getting used to my new rhythm, I was surprised: I was facing one of the castle's sides, where there were people on scaffolding installing something huge that I identified as a handle; that is, they were putting a handle on the castle. A very fat man who was standing next to me said: "It's going to look good, congratulations, it's a great idea." "Thanks," I said, and noticed that I had the handle of the cup I had broken in my hand. I went to my room. When I entered, I wasn't surprised to see it painted all black. Sumenela wasn't there, and that made me think of Ninive, which saddened me. It was noon, and perhaps because of that someone had left me a covered piece of roasted chicken. While I ate it, I realized that I didn't know how to feel about anything. That I was tired but not sleepy; that I missed Ninive but at the same time didn't; that I wanted to see Sumenela, but at the same time didn't; that I was bored but at the same time tired of so many activities. I felt, then, that the other was living for me: he had been in bed with Sumenela during the important moments; he had had that evolution from thought to action with the handle; he had also apparently done something with Idomenea. And that's when

I realized that perhaps his handle was I, that is, that I was the one with a hold on him, and that his wish was to somehow rid himself of me. In any case, he already spent much more time than me outside of the black hole, although it could be that he wasn't ever in the black hole but rather somewhere else, and that the black hole, the void, was a place especially created for me. And I was thinking that surely at any moment he would reappear and I would enter the black hole, when I heard Hugo's voice calling me. I looked out the window and didn't see him. It was a pleasant day, neither hot nor cold, and below, in the garden, hundreds of people were coming and going: women with children, couples in love, groups of men. A little farther on, in the swimming pool, there were lots of people playing and enjoying themselves. And even farther, in the recreational spaces, some people ran and jumped around; I looked toward the forest: a group of children threw rocks at Anibal's son's children, who were up in the trees. Hugo entered my room: "Hey, can't you hear me!" "Yes, but I didn't see you below." "Well, I have big news: Calambra won, now we have another castle, which apparently is huge." "Great . . . Did many people die?" "I don't know, I only know that . . . But anyway, who cares . . ." "Well, great." Then he looked at me: "Are you okay?" "No, not really. This black hole situation is exasperating me." "You still feel it? Ugh . . ." "Yes, it's unbearable." Then we started talking and I discovered that his experience had been totally different from mine, that in fact mine, in addition to being very extended, had been much more painful; but furthermore, and this alarmed me, the other Hugo wasn't that different from himself. "It seems that I'm not that divided," he said. "What do you mean?" I asked.

"I mean that the division between you and your other you is bigger than the division between me and my other I," he said. "I don't understand, you mean that . . ." "Fine, let's change the topic," he interrupted. "Fine," I said. "Look, I found the castle guards' motorcycles, and they're dead anyway, so I thought that we could go for a ride and . . ." "I can't! Imagine if right then I happened to enter the black hole and . . ." "And what? He must drive better than you." "Yes, perhaps . . ." "So? Coming along?" "Fine, let's go."

And we drove around on the motorcycles, had a lot of fun, and at no point did I enter the black hole, which made me fantasize about the possibility that the root's effect had ended. We passed over stone bridges and through abandoned castles; we rested in incredible landscapes, we talked about our problems, etc. And at some point, I don't know why, I started talking about the handle as if it was my thing. And Hugo listened with interest and told me it all seemed great to him; that he had seen the handle being added to the castle and that he had liked it; and that we should somehow transform this theoretical discovery into something that could have a healing effect on people. "Perhaps," I said, a little taken aback by his enthusiasm.

When we returned, I went up to my room and took a nap after eating something. Instead of finding myself in bed, I woke up in the middle of a nocturnal bonfire, because evidently I had entered the black hole during my nap and gotten up. After this surprise, I grew sad, because I was really tired of being under the root's influence; but the sadness couldn't have lasted for more than ten seconds, because what I was doing at that bonfire was presiding over a ritual that, according to a sign, was called "the handle ritual." Hugo whispered in my ear: "Go on, tear them off." It was then I noticed that the people in front of me had a handle hooked to their backs and that they expected me to tear it off. "Okay!" I shouted, and tore off the first one, and I jumped back when I saw blood come out of this person's back. The handles were hooked into the skin; the wound that remained wasn't very big, but it was a wound. I had to remove the handles from seven people, and after Hugo, who apparently co-presided over the ritual, collected them and threw them into the fire. Then everyone shouted, and the women took off their clothes, and the men did the same, and so I, too, had to get naked, and I entered the black hole just after seeing Sumenela among the naked women. When I left the black hole I was still in the same place, and through the chaos of naked bodies illuminated by the fire I thought I saw Ninive, and when I went to find her I entered the black hole once again. Then I left it again, and what I saw deeply disturbed me. I ran away and reached the forest; I sat on a fallen trunk, and seconds later Sumenela also arrived. "Are you okay?" she asked. "Yes, yes . . . No, no, this is unbearable." We were naked, but Sumenela wore a very large shawl. "Come, let's cover ourselves," she said. And so, both covered by the same shawl, we went deeper into the forest until coming upon a clearing in the trees. There we slept. When I awoke in the morning, exhausted but confident that I had been myself and that I had slept straight through, she, surprised that I didn't remember anything, told me what had happened: "At some point in the night you woke up and ran away; I tried following but you were going very fast, and so I decided to come back and wait for you here; some time later you appeared with lots of roots in your hand; I got angry and told you to throw them away, because you couldn't complain about the effect if you kept eating them; you ate them just the same, desperately, and that made you half-crazy and you ran out again; when you reappeared, about an hour later, you were with the castle's previous owner's children; they guided you and told you what to do, and you listened to them; you appeared to have lost all your energy and you kept repeating things about the dead, about the dead people you had seen, something like that." I noticed then that my ankles were badly injured and my hands and other parts of my body very filthy. This explained everything: the effect lasted because the other ate roots every chance he got. I asked Sumenela to tie me to a tree; she refused at first but finally accepted because, according to her, she wanted to be with a man who was only one person. So, by getting me and the other to do the same thing for a while, that is, to be tied to a tree, and above all by preventing the other from eating more roots, I recovered: while I was tied up, I entered and left the black hole many times, and Sumenela made sure to feed me and reinforce the knots every so often; according to what she told me afterward, the other repeatedly tried to pass himself off as me to convince her to free him, but she was able to tell us apart thanks to, as she explained, "a glint in the eyes and a certain little gesture of the mouth." The next day, in the morning, I felt clean; we waited a few hours and, in the evening, almost positive that the black hole was a thing of the past, I asked Sumenela to release me. She looked at me with skepticism, but finally agreed. We went to my room and there we showered and put on clothing that had belonged to the royal couple.

We went out for a stroll, and the people along the way, in awe of our presence, came out to greet us, saying "king, queen." At that moment I felt that even if my other I left, I would keep seeing him, because I had already met him. And suddenly, a woman approached Sumenela and slapped her; Sumenela responded by slapping her back, and so the two began fighting; when I went to separate them, the woman spit in my face. I noticed that it was Ninive, although she was fat and had dyed her hair red. "What are you doing? Just like that, you're back?" I shouted. "Oh, of course: I'm back!" she said. "And who's this?" asked Sumenela. "It's Ninive, my ex," I said, and she, with a sympathetic gesture, ran off to one side. Ninive was indignant; I couldn't understand how she could be so indignant, but when she told me what had happened to her I had to side with her and ask for forgiveness, because it was as if . . . And then I realized that I had to decide who I'd stay with: I looked at Ninive, I looked at Sumenela, and without hesitation, though also without knowing why I didn't hesitate, I went with Sumenela. Behind us, Ninive remained crying. That day not much else occurred. Someone tried setting up a ritual, but I stopped him and declared all rituals canceled. "They were a mistake," I explained. I left the handle on the castle, because it didn't look bad, and because, in any case, I didn't dislike the idea.

Chapter 21

THE FOLLOWING MORNING, I woke up and saw breakfast on the nightstand. Sumenela was sleeping with her mouth open. I reached for the kettle and noticed it was warm. I got up and opened the window. It was a pleasant day, neither hot nor cold, and below, in the garden, hundreds of people were coming and going: women with children, couples in love, groups of men. A little farther on, in the swimming pool, there were lots of people playing and enjoying themselves. And even farther, in the recreational spaces, some people ran and jumped around; I looked toward the forest: a group of children threw rocks at Anibal's son's children, who were up in the trees, out of reach. I thought that I should help them, but I didn't see how. Those children, raised as slave owners, with all of their luxuries and whims, wouldn't be comfortable among us. At the same time, they were very young, and there was still the possibility that their adaptation to the forest would be permanent. Would they, then, be happy? I thought about the wild girl, and as I thought about her my spirits darkened, because I imagined her gray, covered in ash, dry and hard, in a tree top.

And that thought made me eat breakfast quickly and go out for a stroll alone. As soon as he saw me, Hugo ran over to me. "It's not Ninive you saw!" he shouted. "What?" I said. "That wasn't Ninive, it was a crazy impostor!" he answered, now at my side, panting a little. We argued for a while, but Hugo was very convinced. Finally, he confessed that he had seen Ninive's corpse while we buried the dead that first time. "Really? You saw it?" I asked. "Yes, yes, it was her." "Are you sure?" "Yes, of course, it was her . . ." There he appeared to falter, and so I asked him again: "Are you sure, really sure?" He then confessed that no, he couldn't be so sure, because the bodies were dirty and in a bad state, but he was sure that the woman who had tried to pass herself off as Ninive was an impostor. We went searching for her and found her easily, because she had quickly become famous among her neighbors, who knew that this woman wasn't Ninive but rather an impostor who had tricked me; one of those neighbors, in fact, was the one who had approached Hugo with the truth. The false Ninive lived in a hut attached to the castle, so attached that one of its walls was the castle's wall. We called her and she came out. When I saw her, I was surprised at having believed a lie like that: the woman was fat and a redhead, and looked nothing like Ninive. I wanted to insult her and realized I couldn't, and so I gestured to Hugo for us to leave immediately. Hugo wanted to talk about the false Ninive, but I told him that I wanted to take a solitary stroll to think about all this, which was making me suffer, though in reality I wasn't suffering: I only wanted to have a peaceful stroll.

I walked a long distance; along the way I greeted many people, and without realizing it arrived at the bridge and looked down at the stream: it was clean and the smell had almost completely faded. Or was it me, who perceived or recreated a nonexistent smell? While I thought about this, something came down the stream and got stuck right where the bodies had been before. It looked like a corpse, and I stood there stiffly, watching it run aground between some rocks and seeing how quickly the water started to fork. I ran down and saw that, in fact, it was the body of a forty-something-year-old man. I lifted him out of the water and inspected him: he was either fat or swollen; he had long hair and was missing a few teeth; and he had a hole in his head, which seemed to be a bullet wound. I left the body there and ran to find Hugo. Along the way, I don't know why, I asked a boy of about ten to go to the stream and keep an eye on the body. As soon as I saw Hugo, who was gathering flowers with Idomenea, I started insulting him. When I stopped, he asked me what was wrong. "What's *wrong*?" I shouted. "Yes, because I don't understand you," he said indignantly. "You've been throwing bodies back! Into the stream, you threw the bodies back!" "No!" "Yes!" "No!" "Yes! Yes!" "No!!" When I saw how sure he was, I doubted myself. Had I, my other I, been the one? going about this secretly, perhaps at night? I took Hugo to the stream. When we arrived, the child was pointing out two new bodies that had piled up in the same place as before. I looked at Hugo and his face convinced me that he had nothing to do with these new bodies. We took them out of the water and inspected them. They had also been shot to death; one was missing an arm, and another one had somehow lost his hair or had it pulled out from his head. I was looking at this when Hugo said: "Ah! He's one of yours!" "What?" I asked.

"Look." And I saw him: one of the dead bodies really, really resembled one of the four soldiers who had arrived with me and who had gone with Calambra. "They're coming from there," said the kid. "What?" Hugo and I asked simultaneously. "They're coming from there," he repeated, pointing at the stream. " And what's there?" I asked. "The other castle is there." "This stream also goes by the other castle?" asked Hugo. "Yes," said the kid, as we watched three more bodies arrive and pile up in the same place, one after the other, as if . . . We ran back to the castle. We encountered three men and asked them to go to the stream to look for the bodies and take them back to the cemetery. To another, we asked that he go to the conquered castle and investigate what was happening; for this, we gave him a motorcycle. When we returned to the stream we saw that the pile of bodies had grown substantially. "What is that Calambra up to?" I asked, desperate. "It seems that he's throwing the dead into the stream," replied Hugo. "Yes . . . ," I said, thinking that Calambra had learned that from Hugo while at the same time recognizing the face of another one of my four soldiers. We arrived at the castle just as the motorcycle returned. "Well?" we both asked at the same time. "I can't describe what I saw," replied the man. "What?" "I just can't." "Why?" "Because it's horrible." "Many dead?" "Yes, many." "And what else?" I asked, and there the man fell to the ground, and we saw that he had a large, deep gash on his back. We asked a passing couple to take care of him and headed in the direction of the stream. Along the way we came across many people who were carrying the dead on their shoulders toward the cemetery: there were men, women and children, among both the dead and those carrying them. Upon reaching the stream, we saw that the mountain of bodies was already so high that it almost reached the bridge and that, although there were many people helping, it was impossible to prevent the bodies from piling up. "This is going badly," I told Hugo, and instinctively looked in the direction of the mountain range and saw that the gray was darker. Thinking that we deserved the worst, I walked a little more and went up a very high hill; once at the top, I screamed, because I saw what I knew I would see: the ash had overflowed the small mountain range and was passing over to our side. Now a good part of the paradise we had seen upon arriving was covered in ash. I was unable to calculate exactly how long it would be before we were all covered, but I estimated it would be soon. I told Hugo what I had seen on the horizon. He wasn't too alarmed, not even when I took him to the hill to see for himself. The reason for his lack of surprise, I assumed in that moment, was that he didn't really know how things had gone at the previous castle. I tried telling him in detail, but something prevented me, and so I tried convincing him that we should abandon the castle. It was impossible. The punishment of the ash should fall upon us all so that we might believe in it, because I, for some reason, did not know what to do.

Chapter 22

And it didn't take long. That same evening, Hugo and I were going around on motorcycles when suddenly his motorcycle flipped over a few times and Hugo went flying several yards and crashed against some thorny bushes. I ran up to him and helped free him from the branches while he shouted, "Oh, oh, oh, I'm blind," and I laid him faceup on the ground. When I saw him, I was horrified: Hugo had an ash worm squashed against his face. I carefully removed it, and immediately he started blinking. He could see all right, but the wounds from Anibal's lashings had reopened. All the worst, which had been lurking, was now coming back. I told Hugo something about the worm, but he didn't pay attention. He wanted to get back on the motorcycle immediately and keep going. "It's all right," I told him, and then he tried to start the engine but couldn't: the entire back tire was covered with ash worms. Like a madman, he tried removing them, but they stuck to his hands and climbed up his arms. My motorcycle was also ruined, although not by the worms. We looked at it for a while but couldn't guess what the problem was.

"We're going to have to walk back," Hugo said. That meant an hour and a half, at least. I looked at the sky: the ash was rapidly advancing in the castle's direction. I wanted to make him notice the problem, but he shrugged it off and accused me of being delirious: "It's only a storm," he told me. I looked at him in stupefaction. "Hugo," I said, "do you understand what's happening?" He looked at me. He was acting strange, and then I saw a little glint in his eyes and a little expression on his mouth, such as Sumenela had used to describe my other I, and I realized: Hugo was in the black hole; the one who was with me was his other. The problem with Hugo's other was that was not so different from Hugo himself. The only difference, I noticed, was that he liked to get around by motorcycle and that for some reason he desired the destruction of the castle and the death of its inhabitants. This meant that I had spoken with the other Hugo, many times, thinking it was the one I knew. But I couldn't be sure. To prove it, I hit him on the head, which knocked him out, and sat waiting for him to wake up. It took a few minutes; in those minutes I seemed to understand something: that if I was there, going around irresponsibly on a motorcycle while the castle was in danger, it was because through some new means my other I had prompted me to do it; that is, I was acting on his behalf. Hugo woke up, and when I saw his eyes were normal, I asked him what had happened. "I have no idea," he said. "And you don't remember the fall?" I insisted. "What fall?" "And what about the motorcycle, nothing?" "What motorcycle?" "It's all right. Listen to me . . ." And then I told him everything, and he fell into a state of despair. We ran to the castle noticing how the ash went faster than us. Upon arriving, the situation horrified us: darkness, ash, and worms all over, desperate people taking ash out of their mouths and eyes, building little carts to carry their things, crying and shouting. There were, at the cemetery entrance, piles of unburied bodies. They were the most recent bodies that had arrived in the stream; in sum, I calculated, about four hundred. How could they still be there? How could it be that I had gone joyriding so nonchalantly? I ran to my room thinking about my other I. Sumenela was there, looking shocked. "Come on, we have to go," I told her. I looked out the window while she packed some things in a bag: I looked at the pool, covered in ash, which blew in the wind; I looked at the desperate people, running and falling; and when I saw, in the background, the forest, I imagined the three little wild siblings—dry, gray, hardened by ash in a treetop.

CHAPTER 23

How to tell of all that we suffered on our way to Calambra's castle? It was similar to the last time, but far more terrible. And what we suffered after, the few of who made it there, enslaved by Calambra himself, who not only hadn't liberated anyone but had acquired new slaves whom he treated worse than would the worst owner imaginable? But all this was short-lived, because very quickly the ash reached that castle, and we had to escape to the city, where, we had been told, measures had been taken. Measures? I knew that the measures were useless, but what else could we do? And how to tell, then, that new suffering after escaping Calambra's castle pursued by the ash, everyone already totally fed up with escaping from the ash? It was similar to the last times, but far more terrible. When a few us, very few of us, managed to reach the city, the inhabitants were already abandoning it en masse by ship. There I got lost in the multitude, and was now alone. The advancing ash had forced the Navy to prepare the island for total evacuation. No one had explanations of its origin, only false assumptions. In any case, by that time I had become deaf, because the ash had plastered the inner parts of my ears. I managed to board, as a free man, the penultimate ship; below there were still thousands of people, almost all of them slaves, who would not be able to escape from the island; and also thousands of unburied dead, among them probably Hugo, and perhaps also Sumenela, whom I had lost at some point.

As the ship departed, in a total silence to which I had already grown accustomed, I leaned against the stern rail and watched the island shrink away little by little: an ash-covered mountain in the middle of a foamy rain of ash; I saw the three huge and towering columns of fire and black smoke that continued to scatter, like giant chimneys, the infinite decay that I had tried to burn forever in the storehouses; and later I imagined the ship as seen from above: all gray, full of gray, ash-covered people, in the middle of an ocean that would become blue little by little. But what did this mean, that the ocean would become blue little by little? Nothing, in principle. Or yes, something very precise: that little by little the ash was being left behind. To my right, a fat man sighed and moved his mouth; to my left, a woman consoled a crying girl; behind me, someone breathed on my neck. We all watched, up to a certain point, a hazy mountain of ash. Then I felt a "pop" and my right ear unclogged. A few minutes later, my left one would also unclog.

PABLO KATCHADJIAN was born in Buenos Aires in 1977. He is the author of three novels—including *What to Do* (Dalkey Archive)—and a wide array of short stories, poems, and essays. His artistic collaborations include an operatic adaptation of his work alongside the composer Lucas Fagin.

PRISCILLA POSADA is a literary translator from Spanish to English. Her translations include Katchadjian's earlier novel *What to Do*, published by Dalkey Archive Press.

NICHOLAS MOSLEY, *Accident.*
Assassins.
Catastrophe Practice.
A Garden of Trees.
Hopeful Monsters.
Imago Bird.
Inventing God.
Look at the Dark.
Metamorphosis.
Natalie Natalia.
Serpent.

WARREN MOTTE, *Fables of the Novel: French Fiction since 1990.*
Fiction Now: The French Novel in the 21st Century.
Mirror Gazing.
Oulipo: A Primer of Potential Literature.

GERALD MURNANE, *Barley Patch.*
Inland.

YVES NAVARRE, *Our Share of Time.*
Sweet Tooth.

DOROTHY NELSON, *In Night's City.*
Tar and Feathers.

ESHKOL NEVO, *Homesick.*

WILFRIDO D. NOLLEDO, *But for the Lovers.*

BORIS A. NOVAK, *The Master of Insomnia.*

FLANN O'BRIEN, *At Swim-Two-Birds.*
The Best of Myles.
The Dalkey Archive.
The Hard Life.
The Poor Mouth.
The Third Policeman.

CLAUDE OLLIER, *The Mise-en-Scène.*
Wert and the Life Without End.

PATRIK OUŘEDNÍK, *Europeana.*
The Opportune Moment, 1855.

BORIS PAHOR, *Necropolis.*

FERNANDO DEL PASO, *News from the Empire.*
Palinuro of Mexico.

ROBERT PINGET, *The Inquisitory.*
Mahu or The Material.
Trio.

MANUEL PUIG, *Betrayed by Rita Hayworth.*

The Buenos Aires Affair.
Heartbreak Tango.

RAYMOND QUENEAU, *The Last Days.*
Odile.
Pierrot Mon Ami.
Saint Glinglin.

ANN QUIN, *Berg.*
Passages.
Three.
Tripticks.

ISHMAEL REED, *The Free-Lance Pallbearers.*
The Last Days of Louisiana Red.
Ishmael Reed: The Plays.
Juice!
The Terrible Threes.
The Terrible Twos.
Yellow Back Radio Broke-Down.

JASIA REICHARDT, *15 Journeys Warsaw to London.*

JOÃO UBALDO RIBEIRO, *House of the Fortunate Buddhas.*

JEAN RICARDOU, *Place Names.*

RAINER MARIA RILKE, *The Notebooks of Malte Laurids Brigge.*

JULIÁN RÍOS, *The House of Ulysses.*
Larva: A Midsummer Night's Babel.
Poundemonium.

ALAIN ROBBE-GRILLET, *Project for a Revolution in New York.*
A Sentimental Novel.

AUGUSTO ROA BASTOS, *I the Supreme.*

DANIËL ROBBERECHTS, *Arriving in Avignon.*

JEAN ROLIN, *The Explosion of the Radiator Hose.*

OLIVIER ROLIN, *Hotel Crystal.*

ALIX CLEO ROUBAUD, *Alix's Journal.*

JACQUES ROUBAUD, *The Form of a City Changes Faster, Alas, Than the Human Heart.*
The Great Fire of London.
Hortense in Exile.
Hortense Is Abducted.
Mathematics: The Plurality of Worlds of Lewis.
Some Thing Black.